A Man for All Seasons

Mary Billiter

Crimson Romance
New York   London   Toronto   Sydney   New Delhi

CRIMSON
ROMANCE

Crimson Romance
An Imprint of Simon & Schuster, Inc.
1230 Avenue of the Americas
New York, NY 10020

ISBN 978-1-4405-8848-8
ISBN 978-1-4405-8849-5 (ebook)

To Kristen Carter, the best friend a gal could have. Who else would spend her Christmas Day on the phone with me so I wouldn't be alone on the holiday? You understand the tenderhearted and champion for the underdog. You met Ron and knew he was the one for me—even when I tried to convince myself otherwise. You always told me that he fell in love with me over the phone because you watched our love story unfold.

Now as you are about to get married, I get to watch your love story find it's happily ever after. And I couldn't be happier for you and Stephen.

You are my North Star, and there's no other woman I'd want to share my dreams, hopes, and faith beside. And really, have any of your other friends written a book for you? I think not.

Acknowledgments

By the time a reader picks up or downloads a book, it has already passed through many hands and many keen eyes. I am immensely grateful to those hands and eyes that held my book and helped me shape it into a stronger love story.

Tara Gelsomino, I had a lot of questions and you not only answered each one, you continually showed me why Crimson Romance is the team to be on. Thank you. It is an honor to be a Crimson Romance author.

Julie Sturgeon, I've worked with a lot of editors and I even married one, but I've never worked with an editor who knew I was capable of digging deeper and nudged me in that direction. As a result, *A Man for All Seasons* is my favorite story—ever. Thank you. And as far as designing covers—you are the queen of everything!

Annie Cosby, every time your initials popped up on my computer screen, I cringed, thinking, what word did I misuse? What comma did I forget? And how does she keep track of all those rules of writing? Thank you for combing through my manuscript to make it, literally, copy ready! You are a writer's dream.

Dana Volney, my beta reader, a fellow Crimson Romance author, and the overall best critique partner a gal could have. This was such a fun book to write that I figured I was doing it wrong. I sent you a few early chapters and you told me the truth, which is why our relationship works. You said it was funny, light-hearted, and to keep writing. I wanted to marry you. Thank you for being there when it's sunny outside and we're inside writing. Love you lots.

Jami Wagner, this entire story started from a writing prompt you emailed. The challenge? To write an opening scene in 1,000 words. I may have stretched it a bit, but that's my editor's fault. Thank you for opening the door for this story to be told.

DeLaine Walker Britt, when I finished writing this story, you invited me into your summer school classroom to talk to your adorable students about the art of writing. Thank you. You made my summer complete. And now, hopefully, this story will make your winter sizzle!

By the time a book is published, there are only a few people left that will talk to the self-absorbed writer. Those few people make life outside writing a book a true love story.

To my husband, my muse and my man for all seasons, Ron Gullberg. I hit the writing jackpot when I met you. I finally know what it's like to write stories that have "happily ever after" endings because I am living it—every single day. With six kids between us, you still sweep me off my feet. From softly singing in my ear while we grocery shop to being in the parenting trenches beside me, you are a gift from God. I thank Him every day for blessing our lives with you. Gullberg, grow old with me—the best is yet to be.

To my children and my step-kids! Austin, Kyle, Ciara, Cooper, Max, and Dylan—wow. You keep me humble by reminding me that my jokes aren't funny and that I'm the only one laughing. And you all tug at my heart simply by being in my life. I love each of you and I am so proud of all of you.

To my siblings—Suzanne Billiter Cragin, Stephen Thaddeus Billiter, and Patrick Flanagan Billiter—when I can't remember the names of the L.A. freeways I drove for years, you are a group text away. When my sales figures could use a spike, Patrick buys my books to give out as Halloween treats. When I'm struggling to find a funny phrase, Stephen is the king of comedy. When I'm questioning everything, my sister's shoulder is the softest place to land. We are it. And I know Mom and Dad couldn't be more proud of us. Despite the distances between us, we have remained as close as childhood. I love you.

And to my readers—thank you for following my journey and my work. From reporter to columnist to novelist, my readers have been a continual source of support. Thank you.

Chapter 1

"I think I forgot to crack the eggs." My cell phone was propped against my ear as I looked into the galvanized kitchen sink. No sign of eggshells. *Not good.*

"What?" My best friend Kris's voice matched my concern.

"I ... may have messed up." I glanced at the oven. "I don't remember if I actually cracked the eggs and put them in the cake batter."

"Uh-oh."

"Yeah, and eggs are kind of important, right?" I gently opened the oven door.

"Oh, Janey, in baking cakes, eggs are *really* important."

I nodded. Two rectangular pans filled with pumpkin spice mix were positioned on the top rack. "There's only one way to know for sure." I slowly closed the oven door and pivoted on the heel of my boot. I took a deep breath.

"Janey, what are you doing?"

"Oh, you know ... " I pushed up the sleeve of my sweater and reached my hand into the sink. "Just diving into the disposal." The fine texture of eggshells pricked my fingertips. I exhaled. *Eureka.* I pulled out the handful and gently shook it into the kitchen sink. Broken shells scattered. "Yes!"

"Eggshells?" Her tone was tentative.

"Eggshells," I said with a satisfied grin.

"See, you didn't mess up." I could practically hear Kris smile on the phone.

"Not this time." I turned on the water and placed my hands beneath the cool stream. "But me and baking ... " I hit the pump on the antibacterial soap with my elbow. "I really don't know why I keep trying my hand at it. Clearly, I should stick to store-bought."

"Janey, you've got way too much going on."

"I know, but it's John and Jessica's turn to bring snacks to school, and they're supposed to be homemade."

"I wasn't *just* talking about the cakes."

I knew from the drop in her voice my friend was tiptoeing around something.

"The twins would have loved whatever you baked for their first-grade friends." Her logic cut through my frenzied pace and made me smile. "I just think you've got too much going on to even *consider* taking on another assignment for the paper."

"Because I forgot the eggs?"

Kris's laughter was deep and throaty. "No silly—not because you forgot the eggs but because you're a single mom raising two amazing kids and your ex is less than helpful."

"Mark." I rolled my eyes. "He's busy with his newfound wife and their life."

"In your old home."

I shrugged. "Eh, it's nice, but the mortgage payment isn't. Let them have that headache. I can handle this."

"But another assignment?"

Again, I nodded, and the phone almost slid from my ear. I reached for it with wet hands and positioned it back in place. "Kris, if Joe calls and offers me the assignment, I'm taking it." I grabbed a paper towel and dried my hands and the back of my phone.

"Why wouldn't your editor give you this assignment?"

I grabbed my cup of coffee off the counter and plopped down on one of the padded barstools by the kitchen island. "If this were Los Angeles, I wouldn't even have to worry about the holidays and taking time off. And I certainly wouldn't be clamoring for an extra assignment. I was full-time and on staff. I was always over my quota for stories. But, this isn't L.A." I propped my legs on the adjacent barstool, glanced out the window behind me, and watched snow fall on the Tetons. I wrapped my hands around the warm coffee cup and felt my fingers come back to life. "It's Wyoming. And Jackson Hole, no less. There are already *two* competing newspapers here, and I'm writing for the statewide paper nearly 400 miles away. It's like I'm starting all over again, and, worse, I have to find news to report." I took a sip and chocolate mocha perked my senses.

"But that doesn't make any sense. You've been a reporter for like … "

"Easy there, blondie," I cut her off with a chuckle. "I have been a journalist for a while and it's certainly not that I can't cover stories and write the hell out of them. I gave up a great beat in L.A. to follow Mark and his job, but … " I blew out a mouthful of air and replaced it with the spicy scent of cakes baking. "I made the right choice at the time it presented itself. But now? Well, now I'm no longer in a top market for news. And it's kind of ironic. L.A. reporting is like the Wild West, but in the *actual* wild, wild west of Wyoming, it's far more mellow and laid-back."

Kris chuckled.

"It's true. In L.A., the news cycle changes every hour and there's a showdown to see who breaks the story first. L.A. reporters are either quick or they're dead. But in Wyoming?" I shook my head. "The news cycle changes once a day, and that's only to keep the presses from gathering dust. Hell, Wyoming reporters break wind more often than break national news."

Kris's laughter echoed in my ear. "Oh, Miss Janey, that's awful."

I grinned. "But it's true. That's why when an editor hints at a new story assignment, you jump."

"Understood. I just hate thinking of you working on Thanksgiving."

"This is Mark's year to have the twins. Actually, it's our first year to ever do this. When we got divorced in January, I didn't think how the holidays would actually be. They seemed so far off. Now, they're almost here and … "

"Working will be a good distraction."

"Yup. So if Joe has a story assignment, the best thing I could do is work and not be alone on my first holiday without my kids."

"Or … "

The shift in her tone made me grin like the Cheshire Cat because I knew she was up to something mischievous. "Or what, Kris?"

"You could go to where the stories are."

I shook my head. "What do you mean?"

"Well, if Jackson doesn't have anything hopping, I'm sure Casper does."

I half-laughed. "Yeah, and how do I make that happen? They've already got reporters stationed in Casper."

"Yes, but like you said, it's the holiday. Won't the full-time staff reporters be off?"

"Maybe. Most likely."

"So it's the perfect opportunity for you to show your mettle and move up in the ranks."

I wrapped my fingers around my cup. "And how exactly do I go about this?"

"That's easy," Kris said. "Invite yourself over to Joe's for dinner."

If I weren't sitting down, I would have slipped off my seat. "Yeah, I *don't* see that *ever* happening."

"Okay, seriously, don't make me bring up the obvious attraction you and Joe have for each other."

I felt my cheeks burn. "We have a mutual respect for each other's work." I sounded as rehearsed as when I'd practiced, in case the question ever arose with anyone other than my BFF. "Joe is my editor. We have a professional, working relationship. The fact that any time his emails arrive in my inbox I light up like a Christmas tree, well, that's my issue."

"Uh-huh. You've checked out his profile page on the *Wyoming Frontier* website and showed it to me."

"The newspaper has everyone's picture, from the lowly part-timers like me, to the full-time staff writers. But they're in black and white and about the size of a dime. You saw it. It's hard to really know what he looks like. I don't even know the color of his eyes. And our social media policy freaked everyone out about having a personal Facebook page, so it's not like I can check him out there."

"But you would if you could."

"Of course. I want to see what he does when he's not being a statewide editor. I mean, I know what he does because he's told me he hangs out with his son, Sam, but, yeah, I'd like to see that other side of him. But at the end of the day, he's in the newsroom and I'm not."

"But, Janey, you don't have to be in the newsroom to know him. You worked with him before your divorce and after. It's clear that he respects your work. And from the long emails he sends back to you, I think he likes you. And I think you like him, too."

"I like that he's nice and we seem to get each other. He's divorced and … " I shrugged. "I dunno—he just understands what it's like. Or maybe he's being kind."

"Why would you say that?" Her concern came from seeing me through the worst year of my life. From the divorce and finding a new home to Mark's remarriage and reentering the dating scene, it had been hellish.

"I have a lousy track record with dating. And dating my boss? Oh my hell. That doesn't seem right on multiple levels. Shall I count the ways?"

"Okay, okay. But I don't think it's out of the question for you to let Joe know that you'll be home alone for Thanksgiving and that you're available to cover a story assignment in Jackson *or* Casper. I'm sure the paper would cover the cost of a hotel room if they placed you on assignment away from home."

Her logic made sense. The only way my work was going to truly get noticed was by having a front-page story—something I hadn't been able to achieve with the local news I was covering in Jackson. I watched the panes on my kitchen window begin to frost. Snowflake-like patterns covered the glass and created a lacy design. Even though it limited my visibility, it suddenly seemed crystal clear.

"Janey? You okay?"

"Actually, I've never been better." I started to giggle. "Now, I've just got to figure out how I'm going to invite myself to Joe's for Thanksgiving."

Chapter 2

The screen to my laptop was flipped open and a blank email to Joe Argenti was front and center. *You can do this. This is nothing.* My fingers played on my computer's keyboard.

"I've interviewed governors, farm workers, union leaders … he's just my editor," I spoke to no one. Since our dog, Roscoe, had recently passed away, now, when my twins went to sleep, it was just me and my thoughts.

I glanced at the pair of somewhat amazing-looking pumpkin spice cakes wrapped in cellophane. They were ready for tomorrow's class. *I should've baked a third. Cake would give me courage.*

Instead, I positioned my hands on the keyboard and struck the first key.

> Hey Joe—
> Just wanted to let you know that I'm available

I stopped typing. "Yeah, that's not … " I shook my head. *Available? No.* I scrolled my thumb on the touchpad, but instead of clicking on the "delete" key, my thumb accidentally moved the cursor to the "send" button when I pressed down.

"No!" My stomach dropped and my heart rate jumped.

"Crap." I quickly moved my index finger, redirecting the cursor to the "sent" of my email and clicked open the tab. Sure enough, my partial email to Joe was present. "Mother of all things holy."

I picked up my cell phone and texted Kris.

> Just sent Joe the wrong message—literally. Can you come over?
> Need wine, chocolate, and way to fix this stat!

This time when I hit "send" I didn't feel sick afterward. I tapped my boot on the hardwood floor and waited for her reply.

My cell chimed almost immediately.

> OMG. What did you do? Stephen & I r teaching girls how 2 play rummy. If email not happening, call him.

I gently pushed aside my laptop and began rubbing my temple. *Call him?* While I had spoken to Joe many times and conversation came easily with him, this was definitely different. I had just sent my editor the mother of all mistakes.

"Okay, I can fix this. I'll just … " I pressed my thumb into the side of my head, but it didn't stop the throbbing. *Think, Janey. Think.*

I pulled my laptop forward and opened a new email message. I typed Joe's name and his email address instantly surfaced. "I've got this. I'll just send another email. He gets hundreds of emails a day. I'm sure he'll just skim to the latest one I sent and open it. That's what I do with his." It's amazing what the mind will rationalize under duress. I pushed aside the insanity of my plan and began typing.

> Hey Joe—
> Just wanted to touch base to see if there are any assignments that need coverage for the long holiday weekend. I'm willing to travel—in fact, I'd welcome the opportunity to visit Wyoming's central city and file copy in the newsroom rather than by email!
> Please keep me in mind when you're assigning stories.
> Thanks!
> Janey

I hit "send" before I could spellcheck, proof, or reconsider. I had to have this email arrive and jump to the top of his inbox.

As I reread my message, it actually sounded … well, professional. *Maybe that first message will end up in spam. And what's the worst thing that could happen? Joe reads the email. It's incomplete. He won't think anything of it.*

I shut down my computer and turned off the kitchen light. Between almost forgetting the eggs for my children's snack cakes *and* prematurely hitting "send," I had created enough disasters for one day. It was time for bed.

Chapter 3

"So you're available, huh?"

His deep, sexy, roguish voice was pressed against my ear. My body flushed, and I'm sure my cheeks ignited because the rest of me did.

"Yeah, about that, I guess … " I laughed nervously. "You read that email, too, huh?"

"I read *all* my emails."

I gritted through a smile, grateful we weren't Skyping or FaceTime-ing or any other electronic face messaging that was available. It was bad enough he had to hear me stumble through our phone call. I didn't need him to see my embarrassment as well.

"So, then, you saw my *other* message about, you know, possibly covering any available assignments for the Thanksgiving holiday." I held my breath. *Please, please, please.* I would have crossed my fingers, too, but they were gripped around the steering wheel of my Volkswagen bug. I had just dropped John, Jessica, and two cakes off at school when Joe's call came through. I pulled into a vacant spot in the school parking lot. There was no way I could shift gears and talk to Joe at the same time. I was doing enough downshifting as it was.

"Yes, I did read your other email. About that … " His voice trailed off and I closed my eyes.

Just pull off the bandage—it'll hurt less.

"I'm the on-call editor that weekend, and while I would love to have more available bodies for reporting, I'm not sure I can swing that by corporate. It's a far drive to be on-call in the event anything pops up."

I opened my eyes and nodded. "Understood. It was a long shot." *There goes my plan to work during the holiday.*

"But … "

A smile started to form on my lips. *But?*

"Let me talk to Stan, and I'll see what he says. He's the man in charge of the finances and has the final say on the budget."

"Thanks, Joe." *I knew there was a reason I liked you.*

"Don't thank me yet. However, since you're available… "

He's never going to let me live this down.

"My son, Sam, and I always put on quite a spread for Thanksgiving."

"Uh-huh." I purposefully played out the situation. Maybe I wouldn't have to invite myself to dinner. Maybe Joe was about to extend that offer to me. *Maybe, just maybe. The world was full of maybes.*

"So I was thinking that if you didn't have plans for Thanksgiving" —he cleared his throat—"and if you still wanted to make the drive, you could join us. Come meet me in person." His voice shifted to playful and light. "Then you can see why the rest of the newsroom hates me."

I shook my head and laughed. "I can't imagine anyone in the newsroom hates you."

His laughter was deep like his voice. "Well, when you kill enough stories or ask that they be rewritten, you're not always the most popular guy in the room."

I had been on the receiving end of Joe's emails requesting a rewrite, and it wasn't always pretty. Joe was nothing if not direct.

"So what do you think?" he asked. "How would you like to join Sam and me for dinner?"

I grinned so wide it hurt my cheeks. "That would be lovely." *Lovely? Really? I sound like his grandmother. That'd be lovely, Joseph.* Now my cheeks hurt from gritting my teeth.

"It would be lovely." His voice was clearly mocking me.

"Yeah, okay. I don't get asked to, uh … Dinner would be great. What can I bring?" Nothing like a good redirect to move the conversation and my dignity forward.

"Well … " He paused. "How about dessert?"

I silently clapped my hands together. "I can do dessert." *As long as I remember the ingredients, my baking is yummy.* "Thanks." My voice was way too enthusiastic, but I wouldn't be home alone for Thanksgiving and that was worth celebrating.

"Again, don't thank me yet—not until *after* you've eaten my cooking. But Thanksgiving should be fun; I'm looking forward to it."

"Me too." My shoulders raised to my ears. *I don't care if it's the worst meal ever. I have plans for Thanksgiving.*

Chapter 4

"This is stupid."

I heard the rich echo of Kris's laughter through my cell phone. I knew her head was thrown back and her blonde hair swung in rhythm with her throaty laugh. When Kris giggled, her whole body embraced the moment. "It's *not* stupid."

"Okay, desperate? Because Joe emailed that the paper can't justify the cost of a hotel room since I'm officially off the clock. So I can't even use work as my alibi for this little jaunt. Doesn't that kind of reek of desperation?"

Kris chuckled. "Janey, this isn't stupid or desperate. It's … "

I leaned toward the dashboard of my bug as if the closer I got to the front window, the greater the cell reception. Heat streamed from the open vent to warm me and melt the frost that threatened to cloud my vision. "It's … what?"

She paused. I held my breath.

"It's kind of romantic."

Tears stung my eyes. "Really? Romantic? You think?"

"Oh, yeah." The assurance in her voice was a salve.

I slowly nodded. "So driving 350 miles, from one small Wyoming town to another, on … " I couldn't finish the sentence. There wasn't a car in front of or behind me on the two-lane highway. Snow berms, piled high on the sides of the road, didn't hide the fact that the fueling stations and parking lot were vacant as I passed a one-stoplight town's lone convenience store. A red, blinking "Closed" sign lit the window of the neighboring diner. I drove by both without noticing any visible sign of life. "It's like a zombie apocalypse," I muttered.

Kris's voice rose in my ear. "No, sweetie, it's just Thanksgiving."

The knot returned to my throat. The faces of my twin first graders surfaced in my mind. *This is harder than I thought.* "You shouldn't be on the phone. You should be with your family."

"I am," Kris said.

Sorrow slowly rattled my chest. I flicked away a tear, but it didn't stop more from falling. "What am I doing?"

"You're driving *toward* something—toward someone," she said.

"I'm driving five hours and I've never met this guy." I cradled the phone between my cheek and shoulder and quickly wiped away mascara streaks.

"That's not true. You know him. You've known him for years."

I rolled my eyes. "If knowing him as my newspaper editor and the guy I've sent my copy to for the last five years counts then, yeah, I know him."

"Don't do that." She was strong, steady. "Don't discount this. Mark did enough of that for a lifetime."

I exhaled. "This has been *such* an awful year." It no longer felt like pity, just fact.

"It starts over—today. Right now. With this drive, with each mile, you're closer to a new beginning."

Now I laughed. "Well, let's just hope he's … " I paused. *What did I hope? What did I want?*

The sun caught patches of fresh snow that sparkled like diamond chips scattered across the untouched countryside. *There isn't an ugly season in Wyoming.*

"What would it be like to be with a man who had four good seasons?" I asked. "You know, good year-round. I'm not saying that they don't *ever* change, but what would it be like to be with someone who didn't change so much you didn't *recognize* him anymore? What would it be like to be with someone who was consistent?" I paused as the truth seeped into my body and out of my mouth without any conscious thought. "Someone who consistently loved me, whose passion never waned and his commitment never wavered No matter the season, his love wouldn't diminish. What would *that* be like?"

"Does he have a brother?"

Our laughter blended over the phone.

A frost-covered highway sign announced that I would be meeting Joe and his son for Thanksgiving dinner within fifty-five miles. Kris's laughter suddenly seemed farther away.

"Okay," I said in a hastened pitch. "When I get there, I'll text, and then you call. If I feel uncomfortable or, you know, if he isn't what he seems, then you'll help me get out of it, okay?"

"Yes, that's the plan. I'll call you."

"Promise?" Vulnerability caught in my throat.

"Promise."

The phone fell silent. "Kris?" I held the cell in front of me. No signal. I softly smiled and tossed my cell on the passenger seat beside the basket of goodies and poinsettia.

I rolled my eyes. *Baked goods is a given, but a plant? Who brings a guy a poinsettia? What was I thinking?* I glanced at the green cellophane-wrapped divinity and fudge. I purposefully chose bake-free desserts. I wasn't going to risk forgetting key ingredients or having my cakes fall.

In my last email with Joe, he provided directions and a recap of his week. He wrote about his son's band performance and then their stop at the mini-mart for chocolate donuts and milk. Sam had a propensity for sweets and Joe had an adversity to baking them. I grinned. A single dad of a teenager. *My baking will win one of them over—just not sure who.*

• • •

The highway crested and dropped into the city of Casper. The town spread out before me. The silhouette of the mountains rising in the background provided a majestic first look at Wyoming's central city.

I had memorized the directions; still I felt my pulse quicken with each turn and green light that led me toward him. *What if he takes one look at me and reaches for his cell phone? Or he doesn't even come out of his house?* I shook my head, but it didn't erase the rapid-fire thoughts that ricocheted through my mind. *He's not going to think those things. Besides, this isn't a date.*

At this point, self-talk was all I had to get through my first-meeting jitters. *It's not a date, it's dinner.* This prompted a good snort as I laughed. *Yeah, because everyone drives 350 miles for Thanksgiving dinner with a stranger.*

I couldn't help but smile. Maybe it was nerves, but there was also excitement fluttering inside me that I hadn't felt in a really long time. Date or not, I was anxious to finally meet the man I had known only through email exchanges and brief phone calls.

I slowly drove down Elm Street and the two-story brownstone that bore his address came into view. I stared at the faded brick façade surrounded by trees starched in white. Smoke rose from the chimney stack on the older rooftop. Christmas lights blinked from the front porch.

It's magical.

I stepped out of my bug and quickly tucked my jeans into my knee-high boots, straightened my red sweater so that it hung just off my hips, and slid my cell phone into my back pocket. I grabbed my black wool jacket from the car and was mid-inhale into a deep breath when he appeared on the sidewalk.

His jeans were slightly cuffed to reveal black cowboy boots that weren't for show. These were workingman boots. A sky-blue and white striped, short-sleeved sports jersey fit nicely across his broad shoulders and equally well-defined chest. Beneath the jersey, a white thermal shirt with the sleeves pushed up gave him a rugged, athletic look. *Wow, he's really built.*

Sparkling eyes shone from his welcoming face. I felt my heart skip a beat.

"You're here! Glad you could make it."

A wide grin filled my face. *He's excited to see me. He didn't run away.* I draped my coat over my arm and slowly walked toward him.

"Sidewalk's a little slippery." He offered me his hand and it trembled slightly.

He's nervous?

I slipped my hand into his. "You have blue eyes." Surprise clung to my voice.

He leaned toward me. "They weren't always blue." A crooked, sideways smile filled his face like he was holding on to a great secret.

"No?" My voice dropped with just the right amount of curiosity and flirt, which made his eyes twinkle with the brilliance of the lights strung behind him.

"No. I used to have green eyes and I was bald."

I instantly glanced up at his full head of dark hair. "You're teasing me."

"Actually, I'm teasing myself. When I played soccer in college, we all shaved our heads. It was a thing. But," he brushed his hair with his hand, "it all grew back, and thicker."

"And your eyes?"

"That's the real mystery." His tone subtly shifted from humorous to serious. "Sometime after my divorce they turned blue."

"Ahh." I half-chuckled. "I'm not sure if that's sweet or … "

He squeezed my hand. "All I know for sure is that it changed the color of my eyes." He paused and his face softened. "And, I suppose, it changed my perspective."

Joe appeared too tender at that moment for me to ask him to explain, so we said nothing. It's hard to explain why my body already reacted to someone I'd only known through an email correspondence. Standing next to him on the sidewalk with his unabashed wry humor and honesty, a warmth radiated throughout me, like I had reconnected with a part of myself I had lost. But I'd have to lose it again because I wasn't planning to lose my job in the process. *Remember, Janey, this isn't a date. You're at your boss's house for dinner.* The reality was as brisk as the wind that cut through my hair, but it was the jolt I needed to keep my emotions in check.

Suddenly my cell phone rang. His eyes never wavered from mine.

"Is that your getaway call?" He was fun, flirtatious.

"Maybe." I let my phone ring into voicemail. He gently squeezed my hand again. "My friend's calling me, too, you know, just in case."

I tried not to laugh, but it was a battle I lost. Laughter and the magic of the season swirled between us as we held hands and headed into his home.

Chapter 5

Joe opened the door to his home and the rich, deep, woodsy scent of fresh-cut pine captured my attention and hung in the air.

"Like my tree?" Joe reached for my coat.

"Um ... " I scanned the small, but intimate, living room. No tree by the white brick fireplace or matching mantle. No tree by the built-in corner, cherry wood hutch or bookshelves. Nor by the stereo, speakers, leather couch, recliner, or ottoman. No. No. No sign of a tree. It was like a page out of my son's *Where's Waldo?* book. I seriously couldn't find the source of the pine scent any more than I could find the man with the red and white striped cap in a crowd. Joe hung up my jacket and walked to the wall of windows framed by old red brick. On the narrow, white windowsill, a burlap bag was cinched tightly around the base of an evergreen. The tree barely stood a foot high.

I choked back a chuckle. "That's ... " My boots echoed on the cherry hardwood floors as I approached.

He held the tree up like an offering. Pride shone in his eyes. "I cut it down myself," he said with a hint of playfulness to his voice.

The laughter I had held at bay came pouring out. "Did you really?"

His cheeks grew rosy. "Actually, I helped dig it up."

I tilted my head. "And you did this why? So you could have a Christmas tree?" The reporter in me surfaced and the editor in Joe emerged equally as fast.

"Never assume that you know the story."

I teasingly rolled my eyes. "Okay, tell me the story then."

"I thought you'd never ask." He carefully placed his Charlie Brown-sized Christmas tree back on the windowsill. "Remember the piece we recently ran on the conservation effort up on the mountain?" He paused.

The image of a bulldozer clearing debris from Casper Mountain was hard to forget, even buried amid a week's worth of headlines in my memory. "The piece Kelly wrote?" Kelly was the other feature reporter assigned to Joe. She always seemed to get the better story assignments. Kris argued that if I lived in Casper I'd get the front-page pieces, too, but I wasn't so sure. Kelly was ten years younger and ten shades of blonde lighter.

"That's the story," he said. "We were short a photographer so I tagged along and took some pics. The excavator stopped short of this little tree and … " Joe smiled at the potted plant on the windowsill. "I knew it was meant to be saved."

I grinned. "That *is* a great story."

"With enough love and care, this tree will be ready for a tree stand by December twenty-fourth."

"Oh." My voice revealed my skepticism.

Mischievous blue eyes flirted with me, and a swift wave of anticipation whipped across my midsection as if he had touched me and not simply looked at me. "Don't be a doubter."

With a nervous chuckle, I found my voice. "I'm not. I just think … um … " The tree was small, but its spirit was as bright as Joe's eyes when he spoke about the upcoming holiday season. "It's going to make a great Christmas tree," I said softly.

"See, there you go. It's all about staying optimistic. Now you're getting in the spirit."

I'd have to be the Grinch not to be giddy with his good nature.

"And speaking of spirits, may I offer you a drink?" he asked.

"You really are a wordsmith."

"Eh, I'm cheesy that way," he said with a grin.

Despite the fact that I knew I shouldn't appear to be showing favor with my boss, every time he spoke it made me smile. He instantly had an effect on me. I felt happier than I had in a long time.

"A drink?" I inched toward him and tapped my finger on my chin. "Hmm … let me see."

Joe reached out and grabbed me. He pulled me toward him in a rushed embrace. The sudden, unexpected action made my breath catch. My body tingled with the sudden bolt of electricity between us. "What?" I locked on to his eyes, which matched his sky-blue jersey. *I've had a crush on you since you hired me—even if it is ill-advised.*

He nodded toward the ceiling. "Mistletoe."

I glanced up. A hearty sprig of mistletoe neatly tied with a red bow hung from the ceiling.

"That was close," he said with a devil-may-care gleam in his eye. "I usually save the accidentally-stepping-under-the-mistletoe move for later."

His sexy flirtation swirled around me and tingled my lips. Braced against him, all I could smell was cut pine and what I imagined was turkey seasoning that left traces of garlic, sage, and sweet onion on his jersey. It hung in the air for a truly hypnotic hit to the senses. My brain and body no longer functioned in unison. My body responded to his masculine hold, sending both a current of heat and a shimmer of pleasure everywhere. My brain knew I should stop gaping and say something clever.

"Mistletoe?" It's all I could mutter.

"Oh sure. Granted, it's a bit ostentatious, but … " His voice dripped with sex appeal and a roguishness that made my entire body light up in a smile. "The season of smooching starts early in this house."

"Oh." A smile played on my lips. "Well, it never goes away in mine."

Joe's eyes widened and for a moment he lost his hold on me. I nearly slipped from his arms before he quickly reclaimed me and cleared his throat.

"So … " His gaze shifted to my lips and then just as quickly shifted away. He slowly released me. "Um." He ran his hand through his thick, dark hair that spiked naturally. No gel, no slick look—just this haphazard bristly mess that looked touchable. "You were considering a before-dinner drink. What can I pour you?"

"Surprise me."

His eyes searched mine. "Haven't I already?"

Chapter 6

I followed Joe into the kitchen for two reasons. One, it provided an excellent view of his jeans that cupped his ass and hugged his thighs. This man was seriously built. And two, I was trying to discreetly find the bathroom. After five hours of caffeine-induced driving and not enough pit stops, I was afraid that one more good giggle would be the end of me.

But this search was going a lot like the one for the Christmas tree. "Your bathroom would be … "

Joe cocked his head toward the hallway. "Up ahead, first door on your right."

I fumbled for the light, shut the door, and glanced at the wall switch. I literally gasped. *What the hell?* I reached into my back jeans pocket for my cell phone to text Kris.

No fan in bathroom?

I'm not sure if it was a question or statement. I hit send. Any woman on a first or fiftieth date understood the necessity of a bathroom fan. It wasn't a luxury, it was a necessity. Fans droned out sound—whatever happened in the bathroom stayed in the bathroom.

Who doesn't have a fan?

I surveyed the closet-sized space and answered my own question. I could stretch my arms out and practically touch the adjacent wall. The size of the room and the vintage fixtures were apropos for the older house. The stand-alone tub had a shower attachment that didn't look like it'd have enough power to rinse off soap, let alone shampoo. But when I stopped noticing what was missing, I saw the beauty.

Charming, rose-colored tile covered the floor and inched up the backsplash. On the wall behind me, Victorian wallpaper lined the bathroom with scenes of men on horseback and women carrying parasols. I turned and my boot skidded on the tile. I almost lost my balance. *Wowza, that's slick.*

I carefully pivoted and studied the scenery on the wallpaper in greater detail. The men were on a hunt and the women were waiting for them. It was romantic in an old-fashioned, outdated kind of way.

The entire room was quaint, save the fact that the bathroom door didn't entirely close. I gently pressed against it. Nothing. *There's no way I'm leaving the door open.* I pressed harder. The door remained slightly ajar. *I should've stopped at another gas station.* I finally bumped it with my hip and the white-washed door seemed to settle into place and seal shut. A smug smile crossed my face when my cell phone chimed with an incoming text.

Things must b going well! Run water & relax! He's not listening 2 u pee! LOL

The faucet was a stand-alone basin with two antique brass handles. I'd placed my hand on the faucet handle when I heard Joe from the kitchen.

"Oh, hey, the water comes out a little fast," he said.

Okay, I don't need a parent explaining to me how to go to the bathroom. I barely cranked the knob when a geyser erupted from the archaic faucet and soaked the front of my jeans. *Too late.*

I turned the water down to a slow trickle, unzipped my wet jeans, and sat on a very warm commode.

"Heated seat, too." Joe was suddenly running a play-by-play commentary of my bathroom experience.

I giggled. *If this wasn't so pathetic and par for the course for my life, it'd be comical.* When I was finished, I was about to flush the toilet but decided to wait until I was ready to leave. Once the toilet flushed, I knew my freshen-up, regroup, make-sure-I-still-looked-okay time would be limited.

I carefully washed my hands and checked my appearance in the oval-shaped mirror that hung from a rusty nail. Instead of tired, hazel eyes staring back at me, a renewed purpose reflected in bright, actually shiny eyes. *Huh.* My unruly, curly, honey-blonde hair had actually behaved. I only slightly resembled Chewbacca. I tucked one side behind my ear and let my hidden gold hoop fall forward. *Nice.*

When I tried to gently open the bathroom door for a little air, the knob wouldn't turn. I wiped my hands on the dry portion of my jeans, figuring the handle was just slippery. I tried again. It didn't move.

This isn't good. I tried again. Nothing.

I quickly texted Kris:

Think I locked myself in bathroom.

This time my cell phone rang. I swiftly answered it and lowered my voice. "Shh!" I snapped, and her laughter echoed in the small space, which only made me start to giggle. "This isn't funny."

"Kind of is."

I shook my head and my hoop earring went flying into the air. "Oh, no!" I reached for it, but it landed in the toilet, which I still hadn't yet flushed. I closed my eyes.

"What happened?" Kris's voice teetered on sincerity.

"I just lost my earring in the toilet."

Now I could hear her howling, and I was sure she was holding her sides. "So not funny," I said.

She tried to stifle her laughter, but I could still hear her muffled amusement. "Can you reach it?" she asked breathlessly.

"Sure, if I want to put my hand in a bowl full of pee."

I heard her slap something—I'm sure it was her knee or chest, I just wasn't sure which one. She was barely breathing.

Knuckles wrapped on the other side of the door. "Hey, you okay in there?"

"Is that him?" She collected herself. "Is that Joe? He's got a sexy voice."

I nodded into my cell phone. "Um … " I said toward the door. "I think I may have locked myself in."

Kris's laughter exploded over the phone.

"I've gotta go," I said in a hushed voice to her, only I wasn't as quiet as I thought.

"Good thing you're in the bathroom," Joe said in his unnervingly alluring, flirtatious tone.

"Not you!" I bellowed toward him when really I could whisper—the thin, old walls carried my every sound. "I'll call you later," I said to Kris and hung up my cell phone. I put it back in my jeans pocket.

"Joe." I touched the handle. "I'm stuck. I can't get the door open."

"It's okay." His voice was suddenly calm, reassuring. "You're okay. The door's old. It gets caught sometimes. Give me a second."

I nodded and then noticed my hoop earring floating on toilet paper. I cringed. *So not worth it, but will it clog the toilet? Damn it!* I rolled up the sleeve of my red sweater and fished it out. I flung it into the sink, flushed the toilet and, without thinking, turned the water on full blast. The faucet bombarded me again.

I shrieked and tried to turn it off. My hand missed the handle and caught the stream of water. A fast and furious spray squirted me in the face.

I held my hands up. Water gushed from the faucet and banked off the porcelain basin, drenching me and the tile floor. "Help!"

Joe charged the door and barreled straight into the bathroom built for one. I quickly sidestepped, pressed against the sink, and he slipped right past me. Water was everywhere. He slid toward the shower. He reached for me, missed, and grabbed the shower curtain for balance. The curtain, shower rod, and my Thanksgiving Day chef came down with a thud in the tub.

"Joe! Oh my gosh." I extended my hand and fumbled forward. My boots lost all traction. I skidded toward him with my hands out in front of me. There was nothing to grab to stop my momentum. With wet hair and mascara-streaked eyes, I'm sure I looked like Carrie on prom night. The shock on Joe's face indicated I wasn't too far off the mark. The tip of my boot caught the claw-footed tub, but my knee hit the lip and I bucked forward. I landed directly on top of him in the very small, tub.

"And here I thought I was the one who was supposed to sweep you off your feet."

My cheeks tinged with heat and I buried my head in his shoulder. "This *so* didn't happen."

Joe nuzzled his nose against my head, his breath hot on my ear. "It *so* did, and it's one for the holiday scrapbook."

I kept my head down by his shoulder. His silky jersey was cool against my face. I subtly inhaled him. His fresh, clean-scented deodorant had a hint of spice that alone was an aphrodisiac. *Oh, this is trouble.* My body tingled against him. *It's been way too long since I've been this close to a man.* Yet despite what I told myself, I didn't pull away. I wasn't entirely sure if it was the chemistry between us or the cramped quarters that made disentangling a challenge.

"You know, if you wanted to get me in the tub, all you had to do was ask," he said. "I have bubbles and scented soap. We could have made it a party." I couldn't help but laugh. "Seriously, I could get the bubbles … "

I swatted his arm and our eyes connected and our lips were inches apart. *Don't rush this.* I waited for his next move—hell, for anything that would unstick me from a position I was enjoying far too much.

He raised an eyebrow and grinned. "How 'bout we go check on the turkey?"

I hoped a smile dominated my face. "Sure, sounds like a great idea."

"Now," he said, pushing wet hair off my face. "I can't guarantee it'll be as fun as getting stuck in my bathroom, but, we've got to eat—Thanksgiving and all."

In that moment I realized that, no matter the season, no matter the holiday, I would always be wearing a smile when Joe was around. *But Mark made me smile, too.* The familiar pang of comparing my future with my past rose its ugly head and reminded me how slippery a slope it was to even consider Joe as anything more than a friend. When I disentangled myself from him, my feet were on more solid ground.

Chapter 7

My shoulders felt dislocated from my neck and my neck from my body and my body from pain.

"Oh, that's it," I said. Joe's grip on my shoulders released every locked nerve in my body. "That feels *so* good. I hold so much tension all through here." I whirled my finger over my shoulder and circled the stressful region that was suddenly free from stiffness.

His fingers now danced across my shoulder blade. His touch sent a warm rush down my spine that spread across my body like a heated blanket. I was pain-free. My entire body reveled in pleasure.

If his hands can do this to my neck and shoulders, imagine what he could do to the rest of me.

But then the pain seemed to hop shoulders. I tried to turn my head to the right and quickly stopped.

"This shoulder now, huh?"

I gingerly nodded.

It all started after my abrupt fall on Joe in the bathroom. When we dislodged ourselves, a sharp pain shot through my left shoulder and made it impossible to turn my head to the left. Then we discovered I couldn't turn my head to the right when I attempted to glance at the oven timer to report how much cooking time remained on the turkey. Instead of relaying the time, I winced in agony. That's when Joe ushered me back into his living room and onto the couch.

Now I sat between his legs, and it was as if my body belonged there. We melded perfectly. His massively strong hands kneaded my tight muscles.

"Writers get shoulder tension all the time. It's from the computer keyboard, or laptop, taking notes—it all seems to make us hunch forward like we're neck-less," he said.

I chuckled. It was true. My posture at my desk was pure Quasimodo. And as my hair dried into a curl bomb, I even now resembled the badly coiffed hunchback. I pushed the thought of a headful of tossed knots out of my mind and focused on Joe's fingers.

"The drive probably didn't help either," he said. His voice softly drifted around me while his hands continued to lull me into a state of bliss.

I closed my eyes.

He casually dipped his hand inside the collar of my sweater. Skin-on-skin contact. It was a toss-up which I savored more— the tantalizing aroma of a turkey near completion or Joe's hands exploring my back. My senses were on overload. His breath on my neck and then the stubble from the shadow of a beard that had inched across his face as afternoon turned to evening. My skin prickled with pleasure. I leaned my head against his cheek and started to turn into the kiss that was forming on both our lips when the front door abruptly opened.

Startled, I jerked my head and collided with Joe's forehead.

Dazed, I thought I saw stars.

"Wow. That's one helluva header." Joe rubbed his brow. "Ever think of playing soccer?"

I shook my head and wished I hadn't.

"Maybe I should've knocked?" An innocent teenage voice asked from the doorway. I massaged my temples and glanced at the doorway without moving my head. A dark, shaggy-haired, younger version of Joe stood with his hands tucked in his jeans pockets. "Sorry, Dad."

Joe was literally beaming toward his son. "This is Janey," he said, his blue eyes dancing in delight.

"Hi." The teen kicked the door shut with the back of his foot, walked toward me, and extended his hand. "I'm Sam."

"I'm Janey." A firm handshake followed. "But I guess you already know that."

"It's all my dad's talked about."

I waited for some protest, but Joe continued to wear a grin. His emails tended to be staccato and direct. And even while his voice was sexy on the phone, there was no way to determine that he was this optimistically happy guy. *No complaints here.*

"When's dinner?" Sam stared at his father.

Joe shrugged. "Not sure. We were in the process of checking on the turkey and got sidetracked."

"Gross." Sam shook his head.

"Get your mind out of the gutter. We have a guest."

"So, dinner? It is soon?" Sam asked.

"I thought you were eating a feast at your mom's."

"She had appetizers."

Joe slowly nodded. "Well, dinner should be ready shortly."

"Should I pull out the TV trays?" Sam asked.

Joe's cheeks flushed. "No, this isn't our regular father-son dinner thing. It's Thanksgiving. We're eating at the kitchen table."

"We have a kitchen table?" The look on Sam's face was a cross between playfulness and innocence. The kid could really sell both.

Joe swatted the air. "You know we have a kitchen table. It's where you dump all your crap."

I chuckled. "I actually brought some fudge and divinity. It's in my car. Maybe we could nibble on that before dinner?"

"Dessert before dinner?" Joe wore a solemn expression and then clapped his hands. "I knew I was going to like you!"

Sam rolled his eyes. "You're so embarrassing."

Joe shrugged. "Parental prerogative." He leaned toward me and his voice lowered. "How's your shoulder?"

"Better. How's your head?" I asked.

"Nothing a little Scotch won't cure."

Sam laughed.

"May I have your car keys?" Joe asked.

You may have anything you want at this point. I nodded. "They're in my coat pocket."

"Go get Janey's … " Joe softly whispered in my ear, "Did you bring luggage? Or anything to maybe stay the night?"

My body temperature felt like it spiked by a hundred degrees. I turned my head toward him and spoke in a soft undertone. "Um, I did, but I thought I'd get a hotel room. I knew the paper couldn't swing one but I wasn't sure … "

"How things were going to go?"

I coyly raised an eyebrow.

"I have a spare bedroom you're welcome to enjoy," he mouthed into my ear. "And I offer a pretty mean turndown service."

Again my body flushed.

"May I have my son bring your luggage inside?"

"Yes." For a moment, I thought Joe was going to finish the kiss we never started. He looked at me and my gaze shifted to his lips. Then Joe cocked his head forward, and I realized I had trapped him on the couch.

That's embarrassing.

I shifted away from his outstretched legs. Joe swiftly maneuvered his way off the couch and stood before his son.

"Boy! Go get Janey's luggage and the dessert she made." Joe pushed his thermal sleeves back up his muscular arms. "I'll check the turkey."

"What can I do?" My voice seemed small compared to Joe's authoritative command.

"Your jeans are still wet and that looks uncomfortable," he said without apology. "Why don't you let me draw you a bath so you can warm up and I can throw your jeans in the wash?"

"Draw a bath?" Sam's brow furrowed along with his face. "Who are you?"

Joe shot a look that quieted his son.

Crap. *I don't have any other jeans. I have sweats, a tank for bed, a new sweater for tomorrow, and a lot of panties.* I glanced at Joe's teenaged son and gritted a smile. *I brought more of what I won't need and less of what I will. Awesome.*

"If you're low on clothes, I have a shelf full of t-shirts and sweats." Joe seemed to read my mind or my face, I wasn't sure which. "They'd swim on you, but they'd work while we got you out of your jeans ... uh ... " He cleared his throat. "Rather, washed. Got your jeans washed."

Sam patted his dad on the back. "Nice save. Where are the keys? I'm starving."

"Coat pocket and thank you," I said to Sam. I then shifted my focus to Joe. He stood in front of me and his scent wafted around me. Tangy, sweet—he smelled better than the fudge and divinity combined. *What is it about this guy? He's my boss, but he's like this yummy cocktail I can't wait to taste.* I waved my hand as if I were about to say something grand when really I was trying to diffuse the air and the pheromones I'm sure my body was releasing. "Yeah, if I could borrow something to wear, that'd be great."

A satisfied smile crossed Joe's face. "Wonderful. I'll check the turkey and then get a bath started."

Joe had already disappeared into the kitchen when Sam called after him.

"Are we eating only turkey?" Sam fished into the pocket of my coat and withdrew the keys to my bug. "Dad?"

"Sam, have I ever just offered one thing for dinner?" Joe reappeared with his hand on his hip, a turkey baster in the other hand, and a chef's hat that was slipping off the side of his head.

Sam and I burst out laughing.

"What the hell?" Sam said.

Joe's cheeks reddened. "Like it? I found it in the cooking aisle when I was shopping for a roasting pan."

My chest rose and fell with elation and a tinge of sadness. *He wanted this to be special. Mark never did that.* I don't know why my recently remarried ex-husband surfaced in my mind, only that he did. Mark and his new wife were probably in newlywed heaven with my children around their table. *Bastard.* I stood and Joe's blue, blue eyes questioned me as I approached. I half expected him to step away from me, but he didn't. I rose on my tiptoes, straightened his hat, and then gently kissed his cheek. "Thank you."

A startled gaze flickered across his face and then settled into a pleased look of surprise. "For what?"

"Making this first Thanksgiving memorable."

"This is your first Thanksgiving?" Sam was off to the side, a bystander to the moment.

I shook my head but never let my focus veer from Joe. "No. I've experienced many Thanksgivings—this is just my first one as a … " I wasn't sure what my title was when I wasn't Mark's wife or John and Jessica's mom.

"Single woman." My editor finished my incomplete sentence. The awareness settled in my body with an assurance I hadn't claimed. Suddenly, single wasn't bad. In fact, standing in front of Joe in his sweet chef's hat, being single opened a whole new world of possibilities. And they all looked good.

Chapter 8

I dipped my toe into the water. Foamy, frothy, citrus-infused bubbles collected in puffs around the tub.

"It's Tahitian Sunrise," Joe said from the kitchen.

I had quickly become accustomed to the fact that Joe liked to converse through the partially closed bathroom door. It had an *It Happened One Night*, Clark Gable and Claudette Colbert feel to it. Only, instead of dividing a bedroom into two parts by stringing a clothesline, Joe toed the line of appropriate date behavior by keeping a partially opened door between us. And in the off chance he'd catch a glimpse of me naked from between the hinges on the door, I propped the shower rod, with the curtain wrapped around it, in the corner, behind the door. It was another casualty from our bathroom catastrophe. The shower rod was not only cockeyed, It now had a dent from Joe's hand when he reached for it. There weren't any stores open on Thanksgiving, so I couldn't repair the damage, but I could lower myself into the tub and not create more calamity. Bubbles surrounded me.

"You like it?" Joe asked.

"Very much."

"Good. Your jeans are in the wash, and I put some clothes in the guest bedroom."

I heard the front door slam.

A light rap on the bathroom door followed. "Janey?"

It was Sam. *Crap. Does he need the bathroom?* I was so used to my little ones joining me in the bathroom. *He wouldn't do that, right?*

"Uh, yeah?"

"Are there any nuts in the fudge?"

I exhaled. "Nope. No nuts."

I moved the water around with my hands and sank further into the tub, leaning my head against the edge. *Heaven. I'm having dinner with my editor and he's cooking, his kid is eating fudge, mine are probably being spoiled by their new step-monster, and I'm in a hot bath—alone.* No interruptions. I closed my eyes and inhaled deeply. I bathed in coconut-inspired waters, which transported me to a beach somewhere. Like Brazil. They had warm winters. I imagined Joe with his shirt off, handing me a drink with an umbrella floating in it. In my mind, he was about to kiss me when another rap on the bathroom door slowly returned me to Wyoming.

"Janey?"

I nodded toward Joe's voice. "Uh-huh."

"The fudge doesn't have nuts, right?"

"That's right, no nuts," I said with my eyes still closed and Joe's lips moments from claiming mine. Suddenly, I found myself hoping the Joe on the other side of the door would come in and capture that kiss.

"Are you sure?" His voice echoed with concern.

"Uh-huh." Bubbles clung to my body like second skin. "No nuts." The water lapping against the tub was truly hypnotic. I was in a bubble bath haze.

"Because Sam's allergic to nuts and … " Joe paused. "May I come in?"

Before I could answer, he stepped into the bathroom. His eyes fixated on me. "Um … " He quickly lowered his gaze. I glanced to make sure all the necessary body parts were covered. Still, I pulled my knees toward my chest.

"Is everything okay?"

He shook his head slightly. His chef's hat bobbled. "There's an EpiPen in the first aid kit." He pointed toward the cabinet above the commode and walked toward it. "Sam had some of the white fudge … " Joe grabbed what looked like a permanent marker out of the plastic box.

"White fudge?" Now I was shaking my head. "Oh, no!" I started to stand and remembered I really was naked. I dunked back beneath the suds. "That's divinity. The divinity has pecans."

"Dad?"

Joe rushed out of the bathroom. His hat slipped off his head, and in the blur of activity he left the bathroom door wide open. With no shower curtain to hide behind, I felt as exposed as a turkey on a Thanksgiving Day hunt. I scanned the bathroom for a towel.

A hand towel was draped on the sink. I quickly stood and reached for it. *Oh ... that's small.* It would maybe cover half a breast and that'd be stretching it. I placed the towel on the side of the tub and looked for something larger. The hat. I leaned over the tub and hooked the chef's hat with my index finger. I sat back down in the water and held it up. The hat was tall with a wide, pleated band, but it was clearly not enough material to cover the rest of my body. *Great.* I placed the hat on my head and called toward the front room. "Joe? Is Sam okay?" *Did I poison your son?*

When there was no response, my heart rate quickened. *Shit. His son may have lost consciousness because of my baking.* I quickly considered my options. *The shower curtain.* I could unravel it, unhook it from the rod, wrap it around myself, and go check on them. I grabbed the hand towel and rose out of the water. The bubbles had thinned and covered me about as well as feathers do for a turkey. Then the bubbles started bursting as quickly as turkey feathers could be removed. It was just a matter of moments before, like the plucked turkey, breasts and thighs would be fully bare.

I held the hand towel up in front of me and stepped out of the tub. I was heading toward the shower curtain when Joe walked in.

I shrieked and so did he.

"I didn't see anything!" he hollered and covered his eyes with his hand.

I practically dove back into the tub and gathered every remaining bubble around me. "How's Sam?"

"May I open my eyes?"

"Yes." When I looked up, I noticed that Joe's sky-blue and white jersey was streaked with chocolate fudge and divinity. "Oh, my gosh! What happened?"

"Sam thought the divinity was fudge."

"I got that. Is he okay?"

Joe exaggerated an eye roll. "He's better. Sam hates nuts, and nuts aren't too fond of Sam. He had one bad experience with cashews, so we avoid all products with nuts. When we realized there were nuts in the divinity, well, it seems to help him, at least mentally, if he can toss up whatever he ate. So we went outside."

"Oh." Now his jersey made sense, and my heart instantly melted. "He threw up on you?"

Joe nodded and blew out a mouthful of air. "Partially."

"I'll get out of the tub so you can have a fresh bath," I said, but I didn't move. "I kind of need a larger towel before that can happen."

"Oh. Really? Because the bubbles are creating this lace thing on you that's ... " He wiped his face with his hand and rubbed his chin. His face revealed a man carefully contemplating what to say next. "Hell, Janey, that's the hottest thing I've seen."

My entire body flushed and the water suddenly seemed to get warmer. I tried to regain my composure. *How much of me did he see?* "Uh ... does Sam need to go to the ER?"

Joe grinned at my redirect. "No, luckily he only had a small bite before he realized there were nuts."

"I didn't know he had an allergy. He probably should stay away from the fudge because it was next to the divinity."

Joe flung up his hands in a feigned gesture of exasperation. "Yes, my brilliant son thought he could wash the divinity down with a piece of fudge. So instead of just tossing up the divinity in the trash can, it was a lovely mixture of both."

"Oh, Joe." My heart did a slow somersault. It seemed too soon to be swept up by emotions, but from the moment I first placed my hand in his, the attraction I felt for him was undeniable. It wasn't just that he was easy on the eyes, which he was. Or that he was charming and captivating, also true. What really drew me to him was how he parented. He was one sexy single dad.

"The hat looks better on you." His voice awakened every cell in my body, including the neurons in my brain, which reminded me that this was still my boss.

"Yeah, well, I think the hat is the only thing I haven't ruined. It's now official. I'm the *worst* Thanksgiving guest ever. My ex always said my cooking would kill him, but your son was never my intended target." I raised my thumbs out of the water and gave two thumbs up "I'm a real crowd pleaser. A trifecta of awesomeness. Oh, and I'm sure I've caused the turkey to be overcooked."

Joe grabbed the hat off my head. "Oh crap! Not if I can help it." He headed toward the door.

"Towel!" I yelled. "I *really* need a towel." I fished around the tub for the hand towel that had fallen into the water. Submerged in suds, it offered no coverage as it clung to, rather than concealed, my body.

Joe turned and held up his hand. "Turkey, then towel. Give me five minutes."

I shrugged with a laugh. "Sure. I'm not going anywhere. This bathroom and I are becoming very well-acquainted."

He returned, as promised, with a fluffy, white towel. "Janey," he said in a tender tone, "you're not the worst Thanksgiving guest." He placed the towel on the edge of the sink. "I know what that looks like, and you're not even remotely like her. Besides," he said with a wry grin, "look at it this way—what else could go wrong?"

Chapter 9

Joe pulled out my chair and smiled with his eyes. We were identically dressed in Wyoming brown and gold sweats and matching hoodies.

"We look like a NASCAR couple," he joked. "Except you make that look good."

Despite my appearance in his oversized sweats, the look on his face made me feel like Cinderella at the ball.

Sam waited until I was seated at the table before he took his seat. Joe followed with a proud grin.

"This looks amazing," I said.

The turkey had goldened to perfection. Baby potatoes, steamed carrots, and stuffing with a cranberry crust were perfectly arranged in serving bowls strategically placed on the table built for two. Individual wedge salads with bacon and blue cheese crumbles, which toppled down the sides, were stationed next to our water glasses. An empty wine glass waited for someone to pour the chilled bottle of wine. I caught a glimpse of the label. It was some German Riesling that released a woodsy flavor when Joe popped the cork.

"While it breathes, would you join us in grace?" Joe's hand reached for mine.

Our fingers naturally interlaced.

"Sam." Joe nodded toward his son.

"Bless us, O Lord, and these thy gifts, which we are about to receive from thy bounty, through Christ, our Lord. Amen."

Sam recited the prayer from my childhood and that of my children. With my head bowed, I said a quick prayer for my children and imagined their little faces. I swallowed hard, but the ache caught in my throat.

Joe squeezed my hand. "I'm sure they're having a great time."

I bit the inside of my cheek to stop the tears that collected at the corners of my eyes.

He tightened his hold on my hand. "The first year is always hard."

I flicked away a tear with my free hand and tried to shake off the lingering sadness that I had held at bay. "I'll be okay," I said. "It's just weird what'll get to me. Thank you for saying grace, Sam. That was beautiful."

The teen shrugged. "Just memorized it."

I smiled softly. "I know, but hearing you, it was just … " I exhaled. "It made me think of my kids."

"One time I was driving past the baseball field to pick up Sam from practice," Joe said and gently released my hand. He picked up the carving knife and began carefully cutting into the turkey. "I'll never forget this. I saw a woman pushing a baby stroller on the sidewalk and I wept. Out of nowhere."

Sam and I both stared at Joe.

"Why?" Sam asked.

Joe placed a juicy slice of turkey on my plate before making eye contact with his son. "Failure."

It wasn't the answer I expected to hear. "I don't understand," I said.

He resumed carving the bird. "You're supposed to get married and have kids and live happily ever after, then it ends ugly. That woman pushing the stroller had that idyllic life when mine had ended. She was innocently blissful and I was jaded." Joe shook his head. "I was just another divorce statistic."

"Is that how you still see it?" I asked. *Is that what happens?*

"No." A smile formed on his face. "Now I see it for what it was all along."

"Which is what?"

"Loss. It was the loss that made me cry. My marriage was over, and I knew I'd never have any more children. A woman would never be pushing a stroller toward my home."

"Oh, Dad." Sam reached over and patted his father's forearm. "At least you have me."

Joe and I both chuckled. "Yes," Joe said. "I didn't get the house or the car, but I got the better half of the deal—I got you."

I knew from our email exchanges that Joe and Sam lived together and had for the last couple years. I couldn't imagine a mother walking away from her child, but Joe never explained and I knew better than to ask.

"Did you get your kids in the divorce?" Sam asked. His voice was tentative.

I nodded. "I did, and I think your dad and I have a lot in common. I walked away from the house, cars, boat—hell, even the horses—but none of that mattered."

"So why didn't they come?" Sam asked.

"Well, even though my twins live with me, I alternate the holidays with their dad. So John and Jessica are with their dad today."

"When do you get them back?"

I placed a spoonful of carrots on my plate. "Tomorrow." My spirits lifted at the thought. "So is it hard, sharing the holidays?"

His shaggy hair moved back and forth as he shook his head. "Actually it's pretty chill because I usually get two Thanksgiving dinners and two Christmases."

I chuckled. "I hadn't thought about that. I thought it would be easier if one year they were with one parent for the entire day and then alternated the next year with the other parent, but … " I deeply inhaled. "It sounded good in theory, when I divorced at the first of the year, because all the holidays had already passed. But in reality, it's not so great."

"So you'll be alone on Christmas?" Sam asked.

"Sam." Joe shook his head curtly.

"It's okay. Sam's just asking the obvious follow-up question. You've got a great reporter in the making," I said. "Yup, this year I will be alone on Christmas."

Joe stopped carving the turkey. "And miss seeing my Christmas tree all grown up?"

I giggled. "Your dad seems to think the tree he dug up on the mountain will be ready for a tree stand by December twenty-fourth."

Sam's brown eyes weren't like his father's majestic blues, but they held the same current of energy. "I guess you won't know unless you come back on Christmas Eve and join us."

Joe filled our wine glasses and then raised his in the air. "To reuniting on Christmas Eve."

"Here! Here!" Sam said and clinked his water glass against his father's.

Father and son looked at me.

I held my glass toward theirs. "To another road trip."

Chapter 10

"The dishes can wait." Joe brushed his hand over my shoulder and a jolt of electricity coursed through my veins. He reached over me for the plates I had carefully stacked on the table and his breath was hot in my ear. "Besides," he said in a voice that beckoned for the bedroom and not the kitchen. "Guests don't do the dishes. That's Junior's job."

"So what did you have in mind?" I tried to maintain some semblance of balance, but this man made me swirl.

Soft laugh lines crinkled at the corner of his eyes when he smiled. "You can't come all the way to Casper and not see our beautiful city." His gaze scanned me from head to foot. "You're dressed for the weather so I thought we'd take a walk."

My smile was for him alone. "I'll get my coat."

A swift Wyoming wind blew my hair against my wool cap and swept snow off the sidewalk, clearing a path for Joe and me. He reached for my hand and pointed with his other.

"Thought I'd show you the tree section."

I cozied beside him and tucked our entwined hands into the pocket of my coat. "What's the tree section?"

"It's what locals in Casper call this older subdivision because the streets are lined with trees."

A canopy of aspens arched their snow-covered limbs toward the sidewalk. Lacey patterns of frost covered the trunks. The white ice crystals, which scattered across the trunks, caught light from the city street lamps and made it look as though the trees had been dusted with diamonds.

"Hoarfrost," he said.

"The tree trunks?" I asked, nodding toward the brilliant display.

"No, the limbs."

"What?"

"Hoarfrost. It's an awful name, but it refers to the frost that makes the trees look old and aged. If you stand back"—he stopped us—"and look at the frost on the tree limbs, it looks like white hair."

Suddenly, the sidewalks looked as if they were guarded by a sentinel of old men.

"Ahhh … I love that."

A satisfied smile crossed his face before we resumed walking.

"I bet you were a good reporter," I said and my breath hung in the air.

"Why would you say that?"

"Because you're a great storyteller."

Our fingers unfurled and Joe gently pulled my gloved hand to his face and kissed the top of my mitten. "Thank you."

His small gesture was romantic as hell. I had to lock my jaw to keep it from dropping open. When I did speak, my voice was soft. "You're welcome, but my compliment is true. Your story about the woman with the stroller. I could visualize it, but more than that, I could feel the moment."

Another sharp gust of wind blew through us. My scarf protected me, but Joe tucked his chin into the collar of his peacoat.

"Maybe if I had written with that level of emotion, I wouldn't have been bumped to editor."

"Bumped to editor?" My raised voice revealed my shock. "Editor is a promotion."

"For some. But it keeps me stuck behind a desk."

"Oh." My voice dropped octaves. "I never thought of it like that."

"It's fine. I run the newsroom and the features department. I traded one beat for two new ones. So it's not bad. The hours suck, but … "

"That's the life of a newspaperman?"

"Exactly."

I shrugged. "There's always some trade-off, isn't there?"

He glanced at me. "How do you mean?"

"Well, to do the thing you love, usually something has to give."

"What was the 'give' for you?"

"Besides my marriage?"

Joe took a startled step forward. "That's not why your marriage ended, is it?"

I shook my head. "No, but it didn't help that I was always on my laptop or when I wasn't writing, I talked about writing."

"How is that a bad thing? You're a reporter."

"I prefer 'journalist,'" I said and elbowed him. "My degree is in journalism, not reporting."

"Yeah, I can see why your marriage ended."

This time I jabbed him a little harder with my elbow. "Ha, ha, ha."

"You're probably the type who corrects someone's grammar, too." Joe laughed.

"Maybe." I kicked snow that had collected on the side of the pathway.

"Oh, no! You do!"

I could feel my cheeks tinge with heat. "Well, you correct people's grammar for a living."

"Sure, one's a job, but the other is just … "

"Annoying?" I asked.

Joe stopped and again reached for my hand. He placed it on the breast pocket of his jacket. "No, it's cute." He squeezed my hand. "So what if I told you I want you *bad*?"

I smiled tightly.

"Janey … " His voice was playful. "I want you bad."

I tried to pull my hand away, but his grip was strong. I teasingly thumped our hands against his chest. "If you said, 'You want me bad,'" I exhaled through my nose, "I'd say, 'Well, if you wanted me *badly*, you may have had me." I burst out laughing. "Ha. Get it? Badly, had me. It rhymes! And it's grammatically correct."

With our hands sealed together, Joe used his other hand to reach around my waist and draw me even closer to him.

Each time, his sudden moves made my breath catch. *He's so manly.*

"Nope, I want you bad," he said.

My whole body stirred with excitement.

He leaned toward me and soft, warm, tender lips finally sealed around mine and held me in a tantalizing kiss. My chest fluttered and my knees weakened.

Our mouths opened and gently explored each other as snow flittered through the air. Heat rose between us as our bodies responded, asking for more.

"Dad!"

The voice sounded far off, like in a dream, until Joe slowly pulled away. "I think that's Sam."

"Dad!"

I turned toward the sound. Sam was a few hundred yards behind us with his hands cupped around his mouth.

"He didn't have any more divinity, did he?" I asked.

"Are you alright?" Joe yelled.

Sam nodded. "It's the newspaper," he shouted. "They called on the house phone. There's a fire on the mountain."

For a moment, our eyes connected. I had just been handed both a chance to slow this down and to grab what I wanted next for my career.

"I swear," I said, knowing full well Joe recognized the irony of the situation despite our deadpan expressions. "I didn't set the fire."

Chapter 11

"What do you mean I can't go?" I didn't even try to temper my tone.

"Janey, there's a fire on the mountain." Joe opened a drawer in the kitchen and grabbed a reporter's notebook and pencil. The elongated pad fit snugly in his hand. I wanted to snatch it from him and run to my car, but I honestly wasn't sure which back road led to Casper Mountain. And in Wyoming, the locals always knew the way. It may not be a direct route, but it was always the better route.

"And Paul told me it's highly unpredictable which way the fire will turn. The wind and weather conditions are wreaking havoc for the fire crews. He already sent Kelly and a photographer to the scene; I'm not sure we need more bodies up there." He put the pencil behind his ear and tucked the notebook in the front pocket of his peacoat. "Where's my beanie?" He headed toward the front room.

I quickly stole a glance at Sam and lowered my voice. "Who's Paul?"

"Night editor."

I nodded and found Joe pulling a wool cap over his head.

"I could help," I said. "Kelly's a good columnist, but I'm a reporter."

A wry grin settled on his face. "And here I thought you were a *journalist*."

"I am a journalist and that's exactly what the paper needs right now at this fire."

Joe's lips flattened into a thin line. I didn't know his facial expressions well enough to know his tell, but my gut signaled that he was somewhere between allowing me to go and sidelining me.

I held up my hands in a mock surrender. "While I'm grateful for the work I've been assigned, features are not what I'm trained to do. You've read my past clippings. I'm good in the field. I can handle it. I worked in L.A. before this. Putting out fires is what I'm used to. I'm the best reporter you've got under pressure."

Joe slowly rubbed his stubbled chin. "You've got to promise you'll stay with me," he said.

My stomach stirred with excitement.

"You don't know the mountain or the terrain."

This was the career turning point I'd been waiting to seize.

"Janey?"

"Got it. Stay by you. Are my jeans dry?"

Joe's blue eyes took on a skeptical stare.

"Look, I'm not going up there in sweats. I realize this is Casper Mountain and not Rodeo Drive, but I want to look professional," I said "I'm representing the paper."

"Understood.," he said. The subtle shift in his voice made me stop and focus on what he was saying. "Janey, you can't go rogue on me and get caught in a dangerous situation. You have to stay at the media access point and work from there."

"Joe, I'll follow your lead," I said, my voice growing in strength. "But I'm not a novice at this."

He offered a tentative nod. "Your jeans are in the guest room." He then looked over my head toward his son. "Sam, I could call your mom or ... "

"Dad, I'm sixteen. I can stay home alone."

As I rushed toward the back bedroom, I heard Joe's parental side surface.

"Keep your cell phone by you and listen for the house phone. If they lose control of the fire, they may evacuate. The fire could knock down a cell tower, so make sure the landline is charged."

I shut the bedroom door, slipped off Joe's sweats, and slid on my jeans. They hugged my body in all the right places. I grabbed my other sweater, a long, wool, cream-colored cable-knit that could practically double as a dress. But its shape fell perfectly against my jeans and made me look taller than I was at five feet five inches. I pulled my hair into a messy ponytail, which didn't require a lot of effort since my untamed mane had dried into a jumble of curls.

I dug through my makeup bag and dabbed concealer under my eyes to erase mascara streaks and brushed powder across my face to tone down my reddened, wind-chafed cheeks. I was about to touch up my eyes when Joe hollered.

"Janey, let's hit it!"

I took a quick glance in the full-length mirror on the back of the bedroom door. *Not bad.* I grabbed a pen out of my purse and put my cell phone in my back jeans pocket. When I opened the door, Joe was waiting for me. He handed me a reporter's notebook.

"What are you going to use?"

"I've got a drawer full of them. Do you have a pencil?"

I rolled my eyes. "No, but I have a pen."

"You might want to rethink that and grab a pencil."

For a moment I hesitated.

"The temperature on the mountain is ten to fifteen degrees lower than in town—and that all depends on where you're standing," he said without a hint of a joke to his voice. "Ink stops working, but lead will never fail you."

"Oh." The gravity of the unknown hit me squarely in the stomach. *What am I getting into?* "Do I have enough clothes on?"

A hearty laugh erupted from his throat. "Well, compared to your bath—yes. For the mountain, it's hard to say. I've got bib overalls in the trunk that you can always pull on if you need an extra layer."

"The fire's gonna be out by the time you guys get there," Sam said, with the television remote in one hand and a bowl of popcorn in the other.

Joe palmed my shoulder like a basketball. "Ready for your first big assignment?"

I grinned. "Can't wait."

Chapter 12

Heat bounced off pines and spiked the temperature on Casper Mountain. The media access point was a tight, blocked-off area we hiked to from the makeshift parking lot the fire crews set up on the mountain. Even from the safe distance of the cordoned media point, the fire seemed to burn up the air.

"It's suffocating," I said under my breath.

"Write that down. I want readers to get a *feel* of this fire," Joe said and pointed toward the fire battalion chief. "Charlie Gambino. He's a good guy but—"

"Don't ask stupid questions." Her blonde mane and raspy, Demi Moore-like voice made an appearance before her lanky frame came into view and saddled up beside Joe. "Hey, boss."

Kelly Coulter. Her newspaper column picture didn't do her justice. She was actually blonder, thinner, and her eyes a more radiant shade of blue. They focused with laser sharpness when she cocked her head toward me.

"Who's the new girl?" she asked.

"I'm Janey. We share the features page," I said in my best attempt at humor, only my throat was dry so my voice sounded flat and dull.

"Janey?" A quizzical look crossed her steely blue eyes. "Oh, *you're* Janey Miller? You don't look anything like your photo."

That's what every girl wants to hear. "Yeah, it's five years old. And actually, it's Turner now. Janey Turner." I could've said I was Tina Turner for the response it elicited in Little Miss Sunshine, who clearly showed no interest. *I get it. I'm on her beat; I'd be territorial, too.*

"Uh-huh." Her position next to Joe didn't give either of them much space to move, let alone breathe. She situated herself so

I couldn't see his face or reaction. "What's *she* doing here?" she asked. "I thought she lived in some Godforsaken place like Star Valley, or something."

Does she actually think because she turned her back to me that I can't hear her?

"She lives in Jackson Hole, and I invited Janey to join Sam and me for Thanksgiving." Joe smiled toward me before Kelly quickly tilted her mane, again blocking my view.

What the hell?

"So did you think I'd need backup for this fire?" She wagged her finger back and forth like she was schooling Joe. She coyly looked at me over his shoulder and smiled. "Joey, you know I can handle the coverage—alone." I felt my stomach drop. *Please don't play favorites, and if you do, pick me.*

Joe took a step away from Goldilocks. "Team coverage is crucial to any fire. I'm grateful Janey was in town to join us." He looked at me. "Her beat in Jackson gets pretty quiet, but her reporting skills are solid."

Joe kept looking at me until I smiled.

"Okay," he said. "Janey, Chief Gambino is going to hold a press conference at the top of the hour, which isn't far from now."

I pulled out my notepad and started taking notes.

"I'd like you to cover the press conference and then talk to the chief. Find out what he's *not* telling the other news outlets." Joe turned toward his conjoined twin. "Kelly, I'd like you to talk to the locals. Find out which families were affected. If there's an investigator on the scene, locate him or her and—"

I cut him off. "Investigator? Joe, shouldn't I be covering that along with Chief Gambino?" I rapidly tapped my pencil on my pad. "I'm sure he'll be making an announcement in his press conference. I could follow up, and that would leave Kelly more time to canvas the neighborhoods."

"That's kind of you to offer, but while you're scribbling down what the chief says, I'll be working the backstory," Kelly said with a flip of her hair and a wave of her smartphone. "You don't know this mountain or the locals the way I do."

Joe slowly nodded. "I've got to go with Kelly on this one. She has a local connection to how this fire is impacting the community and who it involves. She'll spot the investigator before the chief even points him or her out, by the mere fact that Kelly was born and raised in Casper."

"No problem," I said through a clenched jaw. "I'll work the front line and let Kelly work behind me." I flashed a grin her way. *Two can play this game.*

She may have been a triple threat—tall, blonde, and blue-eyed—but she was one threat I wasn't willing to let steal my byline.

Suddenly, a crack made me look up. We all did. Fire stretched high into the night sky from the tips of pines ablaze in flame. If the fire didn't consume the mountain, the melting snowpack would. The forest was in danger, and it was closing in on the mountain community.

My petty emotions paled to what these families were experiencing. It was Thanksgiving—a time to be grateful, the season of giving. I saw families evacuating their homes with nothing more than the clothes on their backs and frightened looks on their faces.

"Joe, I'll go wait for the chief's press conference and report back to you. Where will that be?" The sincerity in my voice was palpable.

"Go to my truck. I'll have my laptop ready for you to start filing copy. We may not have an Internet connection, but you can begin writing," he said.

"Got it." I headed toward the top of the media access area.

"Janey."

I turned.

Joe's sky-blue eyes framed his face and held me. "Be careful."

Chapter 13

In Wyoming, the period of time between seasons is often referred to as a "tweener." As I witnessed the ease between Joe and Kelly as they worked together and their conversation, which was a shorthand all its own, I, too, felt somewhere in between. *Do we have that kind of connection?* I was in a tweener of emotions that was absolutely awful.

I stood behind the flashing orange and white barricade that was about twenty feet away from them. The barrier had been set up to keep reporters at a safe distance from the fire. The fire had less chance of burning me than their interaction. It ignited a feeling I hadn't expected: envy. It wasn't just that she was getting time with him, it was that she seemed to get him. She spoke Joe's language, and I wasn't fluent.

I turned my attention to the pending press conference. I wasn't about to leave my post to go sidle up beside Joe and stake my claim, though the thought had crossed my mind. I had a coveted spot at the front of the crowd with a growing sea of reporters behind me. I rubbed my forearm, but it didn't stop the penetrating heat that radiated from the fire and felt as though it were burning through my sweater. My heavy wool coat was in Joe's truck, and I was beginning to wish I had left my sweater there, too.

Charlie Gambino was a stout man with broad shoulders and a barrel chest. With the fire as his backlight, his dark brown eyes and hardened stare cast a foreboding that I couldn't even begin to craft into words.

Pine trees looked like lit matchsticks against the hazy western sky. Combined with the silhouette of the chief against the flaming backdrop, it had a real *Gone with the Wind*, Atlanta-burning-to-the-ground feel. I knew I was looking at the lead to my story. I leaned toward Alan, the photographer Joe had assigned to me, and whispered, "I think that's our cover shot."

He nodded and moved into position.

Joe wants the readers to feel this. I tapped my teeth together. *How do I do that?* The ground, which had recently been frozen and covered in snow, was now slick with mud. The mountain was literally losing ground. A mudslide could easily happen. I was standing in a moment in history. The rapidly spreading fire could change the landscape of Wyoming's central city.

The chief cleared his throat. I glanced toward him. He grabbed a bottled water stuck in the pocket of his fire pants. He took a swig, and I understood. There was no moisture in the air. Smoke clouded the sky and burned my eyes. The fire was consuming everything.

"Okay, folks," he began. "We're going to make this brief because … " He paused. "Well, quite frankly, we need every available body to work this fire."

The veteran fire chief didn't have a prepared statement, nor did he have a public information officer standing at the ready. All of Wyoming paled in population to other states and even large metropolitan cities, like neighboring Denver. I quickly scrolled my phone for Internet service and discovered the magnitude of this fire.

I jotted figures on my notepad. Casper Mountain was more than ten square miles, but it covered about 56,000 acres. *With lodgepole pine that ignites like kindling. Holy hell.*

"They can't do this alone," I said to no one in particular. "They'll lose the mountain—not to mention the cabins. Where will everyone go?"

The gravity of the fire sent a chill down my spine. I glanced back to find Joe, but I couldn't see over the crowd. *I wish he were here with me.*

"How big is your crew?" a reporter yelled over the drone of the fire engines.

"Our fire personnel is roughly 350," the chief said.

A collective gasp followed. The Casper Fire Department was not equipped to handle a fire of this size without additional help.

"What caused the fire?" The question shot out of my mouth. It was the most rudimentary question a freshman reporter would ask, but that didn't negate its importance. The answer would direct the focus of my story.

"Lightning." The fire chief took off his helmet and wiped his forehead with the back of his arm. "We received reports of lightning throughout the night." He tucked his helmet beneath his arm. "However, there weren't any reports of fire until late this afternoon. The lightning squall started a series of fires on the face of the mountain that has grown to about two football fields in length."

While I could visualize this, I needed specifics. *Joe wants readers to feel this, and Wyomingites know acreage.* "How many acres have burned?" I asked.

"Thirty acres so far."

"What are your crews doing to control the fire?" another reporter asked.

"We've focused our suppression efforts on the ground. There's a layer of fuel beneath the trees—juniper, sage brush, and subalpine fur—and it sits like a fuse with the potential to burn from the ground to the top of the trees. By containing that layer, we're hopeful these fire suppression efforts will prevent further burn areas," the chief said earnestly.

"How is that area suppressed?" another reporter called out.

The chief pointed toward the ground. "We soak it. We drench it with water and keep it wet."

"Won't the temperatures freeze the water before it has the ability to do its job?" someone asked.

"Normally in November, yes, but the fire has dramatically increased the temperature on the mountain, so freezing isn't an issue," he said. "At least, for now."

Suddenly, the slick mud beneath me was a welcome relief. The distinct buzz of helicopter blades cut through the night.

"Chief, is that reinforcement?" an anonymous voice asked from the crowd.

"The National Guard assigned two Black Hawk helicopters and two single-engine air tankers to the fire. The steep and rugged terrain of this mountain has forced my crew to build containment lines by hand until we can get bulldozers up here. The air tankers will hit those areas in the middle that we can't access."

"Has the fire claimed any homes?" I knew I was jumping in on Kelly's turf, but I had to know.

The chief looked at me. His brown eyes conveyed the message before he spoke. My stomach dropped. "The fire took two cabins, a barn, and an outbuilding."

"Were any occupants injured?" I followed up.

He shook his head curtly. "No. The homes were vacant."

It was the only good news of the night. And suddenly the oddest question popped out of my mouth. "Chief, how old is this forest?"

This time his eyes warmed back at me. "The forest on Casper Mountain is 130 years old. My father worked this mountain and his father before him. This forest has been here longer than most generations and shares more history with this town than any archive you'll find in our library."

The chief placed his helmet back on his head and nodded toward the crowd. "We'll keep you updated throughout the evening." He then turned and disappeared behind the barricade into a cloud of smoke.

The crowd of reporters dispersed quickly. I found Alan behind the hordes of onlookers, aiming his camera into the night sky as another helicopter buzzed by.

"Get anything good?"

Alan nodded. "What about you?"

I shrugged. "I got everything everyone else got. I couldn't talk to the chief afterward. I don't have anything *new* to report." *I let Joe down.*

"But you have the basics," Joe's voice came from behind Alan.

Joe's scent cut through the thick, burnt wood and his aroma surrounded me. My shoulders dropped and so did my defenses. *Maybe I didn't blow it. I could add some historical reference to the age of the forest and who knows what else. It's not over yet.*

"Listen, all these pieces go together to build our story," Joe said.

"Our story?" I scratched my head. "Am I writing this piece with Kelly?" *Isn't it bad enough she's cutting in on my Thanksgiving byline?*

"Kelly's already at my truck writing. Your notes will build into her piece."

"Oh." If the fire hadn't already made it painful to breathe, Joe's announcement would have.

Joe and Alan were waiting on me to respond. My reaction was crucial. Balk, and I'd be back to features for sure. *Cowboy up, Janey. A front-page byline is still a front page.*

"Great. I'll go meet up with her and give her my notes." I pivoted to leave and felt my boot catch in the mud. *Easy does it. All I need now is to fall on my ass.* A hollow emptiness engulfed me as I made my way toward Kelly and the truck. I kicked a rock and watched it careen down the mountain. *I did let him down and Kelly didn't.* I reached down and grabbed a pinecone that hadn't lost its shape. *Let's think this through.* I held the rough pinecone and rubbed my thumb across its accordion-like structure. *I could blame Kelly for doing exactly what Joe knew she'd do, which was get the locals to talk.* The coarse scales pricked my fingers. I chucked the pinecone as far as my throwing arm, which was still sore from when I landed on Joe in the bathroom, would allow. *Or I could figure out a different angle to this story and wow them both.*

I scuffed the tip of my boot on the craggy mountainside, trying to dig up another rock or something to hurl. Instead, I found more pinecones. *Or there's always the third option. The twins and I could make Christmas trees out of these little pine nuggets and I could start writing a craft column for the paper.*

I glanced up the mountain. I was far enough away from the fire danger; my only real danger was of losing myself in self-pity.

I'm thinking the wow factor is in order.

I went around picking up as many pinecones as the bottom of my outstretched sweater would hold. I held up one. "This may be one of the last relics from this mountain," I said and then shook my head. *And that may be the last original thought I have before I meet up with Kelly to hand her my notes.*

At some point, I zigged when I should have zagged because soon I realized I couldn't see the makeshift parking area.

"Awesome." Kelly was burning the midnight oil with Joe, and I was just burning time. I continued to wallow when he appeared out of nowhere.

"Lost?" The unfamiliar voice startled me.

I jumped. Pinecones flew in the air like wild turkeys startled by a pilgrim's musket shot. In my befuddlement, I not only surrendered my sweaterful of souvenirs, I forfeited my foothold against the muddy terrain. I began to tumble when he reached out and grabbed me. But the ground was too slick and I continued to lose traction. Suddenly, I saw the jagged grade of the mountain, and it wouldn't be a friendly fall.

"Oh, no!" I tried to hold onto his hand, but my palm was slick with pinesap and slipped away from his. He braced his leg against the shoulder of the mountain, scooped me up into his arms, and swiftly carried me to a small plateau further down the side of the rocky terrain.

"Who are you?" I asked, breathless and curious. "And where are all my pinecones?"

The brim of his cowboy hat shielded his face.

When he set me back down on the ground, I saw older eyes the color of the evergreens before they had ignited.

"Thank you," I said.

"Nothing to thank." His voice was edgy and rough. "Just happened to be at the right place, at the right time." He tilted his head, and the angle brought his entire face into view. Deep-set, green eyes that seemed to size me up softened when he asked, "You know where you're going?"

I chuckled. "I only *look* lost. I'm heading toward the parking area thingy."

Now he laughed, and it was deep and robust. "Then you'd better head north."

"Ohhh-kay." I gave two thumbs up.

"You don't know which direction north is, do you?"

I shook my head. "Nope. No clue." I can dodge through lanes of L.A. traffic, weave between semis and sedans to merge at the last second from one multilevel California freeway to another, but somehow, even with GPS or this seasoned Wyomingite in front of me, I still manage to get lost on a one-way Wyoming mountain road. *What the hell is wrong with me?*

His gaze zeroed in on me. "When you're in town, the mountain is always south. So when you're on the mountain … "

I leaned toward him, waiting for him to finish his sentence, when I realized he was expecting me to fill in the blank. "Right. So … if I head toward the town … then the town is always … north. It's north."

When he smiled, a dimple appeared on either side of his mouth. "You got it."

I pumped my fist into the air that billowed with smoke. Trees covered my line of vision. I grabbed my notepad out of my back pocket and used it as a visor to shield my eyes from the overhead smoke, but it didn't work. I glanced back at the cowboy. "What if you can't see the town?"

"Follow the slope of the mountain. It'll take you north."

"So if I keep going down, I'll hit the truck?"

He began to laugh again. "Well, hopefully, you won't hit anyone's truck," he said.

No, but I may hit Kelly.

"So," he said. "If you keep heading north, you'll find the temporary parking lot."

And Joe. I want to find my way back to Joe. I exhaled. "Thank you. You're a real lifesaver."

"Just helping out." He had the look of 100 percent pure western, Wyoming romance, and he wore it well with the cowboy hat, faded jeans, denim jacket with rolled up cuffs, and a can of dip in his front pocket. But my quirky guy in a chef's hat still looked better "So where's your horse?" I teased my rescuer.

"She's in town at a friend's barn." The somberness of his tone brought me back to reality.

"Of course. The fire." I flung my hand in the air and accidently tossed my notepad. I scrambled toward it but he deftly caught it midair before it landed in mud. He handed it to me.

"Well, I'm just a mess." I brushed debris from my notepad against my jeans. "I'm supposed to get something exclusive about this fire, and I've got"—I flipped through the pages—"nothing. Zip. Nada. I'll never land ... " *Joe or my own front-page byline, ever.*

I blew out a mouthful of air. "Yeah, too much information, which is ironic because I don't have enough information here." I flapped the notepad shut and stuck it in my back pocket beside my cell phone. "Hey, thanks for all your help." I turned to leave, when his voice called out after me.

"It hasn't burned like this in seventy years."

"What?" I turned back and loose strands of my hair hit me in the face. "What do you mean?" I tucked a curl behind my ear.

"The last big fire we had on the mountain was about seventy years ago. Wildlife walked around the streets. Moose. Deer. Antelope. Brown bears were even spotted in town by the theater."

"And you would know this, how?" The reporter in me surfaced.

"My grandparents."

Before he could continue, I stretched out my hand. "I'm Janey Turner with the *Wyoming Frontier*."

"I'm Frank Outterland."

"Outterland? Isn't there an exit off the highway named 'Outterland'?"

He nodded. "My grandparents, Bob and Louise Outterland, were married just after World War I ended and had one of the first homes on Casper Mountain. That exit was named in honor of them."

I pulled out my notepad and began writing… "And this fire you mentioned, it happened in what … " I quickly did the math on the page. "1944?"

"Yup, that's about right. It happened during the war," he said.

"What caused that fire?"

A wry grin filled his face. "Lightning."

"Nuh-uh." I tilted my head toward him. "Are you putting me on?" *Did Kelly put you up to this?*

"I'd let you see their photo albums and the newspaper stories about the fire and the wildlife on the streets, but … " His voice trailed off.

I stopped taking notes and looked up. His green eyes watered in a camouflage of color. "Their home didn't survive this fire."

I slapped my hand to my chest. "Oh, no." A wave of grief settled over me. "I'm so sorry." I thumbed back a few pages to the press conference notes with Chief Gambino. "So their home was … " I paused. The reporter in me realized the only way I could quickly vet this source was to see if his notes aligned with the press conference. But even then he could have been in the crowd and heard this information.

"My grandparents had a cabin," he said. "And my parents had the neighboring cabin. Neither of their homes survived."

"I'm so sorry for your loss. This must have been a hard Thanksgiving for you."

He half-laughed. "We usually spend one of the holidays up at the cabin." He glanced toward the upper portion of the mountain that glowed from a distance. "But we decided to wait until after Thanksgiving. Now, we can't … "

I kept my pencil on the page during the pause. My gut tightened with the keen awareness that he was about to reveal something big.

Instead, he reached into his back jeans pocket and withdrew a red bandana. He wiped his brow and repositioned his hat. "There was a radio in my grandparents' cabin that I wish I could've saved."

Any question I had about the fire vanished from my mind as his story unfolded. "It was on that radio that my grandparents heard that the United States had declared war on Germany. The next day my uncle enlisted." He tucked the bandana back into his pocket and his eyes seemed to fade to a memory he had stored in the back of his mind.

"My grandmother sewed a flag that they hung in the window of their cabin. Mothers of servicemen did it back then to show support. It had a star for each family member serving in the war. A blue star represented a living serviceman. Her flag had one blue star." His strong voice began to disappear.

I stood silently in the shadows of his grief.

"They didn't get many visitors up on the mountain back then," he continued. "So the sight of a Western Union man walking up the dirt road was something they never forgot."

"Your uncle?" My voice was barely audible.

He nodded. "He was killed in Italy. Damnedest thing. Mussolini had fallen and Italy had surrendered, but there were still some hot spots, and he ended up in one of them. They placed that telegram in their Bible and that's where it remained all these years." Pain riddled his face, but he had a story to tell. "Before they even got my uncle's body back, my grandmother sewed a new star on her flag."

"Why?"

"Those who lost their lives in the war became gold stars; moms of fallen soldiers became known as Gold Star Mothers. Do you know they still recognize these women?"

I slowly shook my head.

"Sometime in September—right before the rush of the holidays. We always put a bouquet with a gold ribbon on my grandmother's grave to remember what she lost in the war, too."

I exhaled, but my lungs felt tight.

"You know, what really gets me," he said, and his voice suddenly sparked, "is that their little cabin survived that first big fire and that was *well* before there were paved access roads leading up to the mountain."

"So this fire happened in 1944?"

"A year after my uncle died and two years after war broke out. That cabin meant everything to my grandmother, and I think that's why my grandpa fought like hell to save it. He was a tough old bird. The fire crews came and told him to get out because the fire could be there in a matter of minutes. Instead, he sent his three children and wife down the mountain with them and he fought the fire. The fire was taller than the pine trees. Still, he threw buckets of well-water on the roof of his cabin while the fire blazed around him."

"He sounds like he was an amazing man," I said.

"He was," another voice answered.

I turned toward the gravelly voice behind me. "Chief Gambino?"

"We had reports of stragglers on the west side of the mountain." The chief's voice was nearly hoarse.

"I just haven't been able to leave," Frank said. "I came up late this afternoon and started pouring buckets of water on their cabin roof, but I couldn't save their home or my parents' ... "

The chief gave Frank a hearty slap on the back. "We had to make you evacuate. It was too dangerous. I'm sorry we couldn't save your homesteads."

"Chief, can you verify the owners of the two cabins that were lost in this fire?" I asked with pencil poised. *Joe's going to ask me this anyway. The man loves his details.*

"We haven't released that information," he said, no doubt fully aware that I already knew the homeowners' identities. Still, the chief was following protocol. "Until we inform the family ... "

"Charlie, it's okay. I think it'd be great if their story could be told," Frank said.

The chief smiled slightly. "Fair enough. The first cabin was the home of the late Dr. Bob and Louise Outterland, and the other was home to their son, Robert Jr., and his wife, Mary."

"And there were no occupants in the homes at the time of the fire?"

"That's correct," the chief said.

"Chief, is it true the fire that happened nearly seventy years ago on this mountain also started by lightning?"

"Yeah, that's true as well," he said. "When the lightning struck, it hit hard. The fire started on the backside of the mountain and burned for days that rolled into a week."

"I had no idea," I said.

"Maybe that's the scoop you needed for your story. Granted, it's not *new* news, but it's a piece of history that ties into this story that most folks around here would appreciate," Frank said. "And those who don't know the history will now."

It felt like my heart dropped to my stomach. "My rant about this story was stupid, especially with everything you have going on. I can't believe you stopped to tell me all of this."

He smiled beneath his cowboy hat. "It seemed like your luck was about to change."

I swallowed, but the lump in my throat remained. "Thank you. That was unbelievably kind of you." I then shook hands with the chief. "And thank you. I write for the *Wyoming Frontier,* and I'm not as familiar with this area, its people, or the history."

"Thank me by getting safely down to your vehicle and heading off the mountain. Unless we have an early Christmas miracle, we're going to lose the mountain. This fire isn't going to be contained any time soon," the chief said.

"Is there any way I could snap a picture of you two before I leave?" I knew I was pressing my luck, but this story needed a visual. I grabbed my cell phone and quickly held it up. "Please? I promise you'll never hear from me again."

The chief rolled his eyes. "If only that were true," he said and elbowed Frank. "Come on, gorgeous, let's give this news gal a picture."

The two men looked somber against the flame-ridden backdrop. I pressed the button on my cell phone and snapped away in rapid succession. I captured them posed and then as they both turned to look at the damage the fire had left in its wake.

The chief shook hands with Frank and then left as quietly as he had arrived.

"Thank you for sharing your story with me," I said to Frank. "I can't even imagine your loss."

"I'll keep a lookout for your story *and* your pinecones," he said with the hint of a smile.

I felt my cheeks flush. *Pinecones.*

"Who knows," he said. "Maybe your story can start a new album of memories for my family."

There was a moment of silence between us when everything Frank couldn't convey about the loss of his family's homes showed on his face. I could see memories in his eyes, and sorrow filled the lines around his clenched jaw. I wanted to reach out and touch him or hug him, something to make it better, but his stance was one of solitude.

"I've got a great story to go write," I said softly. "I better get to that computer."

"Be safe," Frank said and turned toward the face of the mountain.

"You, too," I said and walked in the opposite direction. After a few minutes, I looked up the mountain. The cowboy had disappeared from view.

Chapter 14

A temporal sky broke in a strike of lightning. I scurried toward Joe's truck. He was in the front seat and leaned over to open the passenger side door. It swung out and I almost bumped right into it. My adrenaline was on overdrive. I hopped into his truck and closed the door.

"Where have you been?" He pulled me toward him and wrapped his arms around me. "I was about to send out search and rescue for you." He hugged me tightly, and I relaxed beneath his strong hold.

"I met a cowboy up on the mountain."

When he pulled away from me, the ghost of his cologne lingered on my sweater. "I thought I was your Thanksgiving date. If cowboy hats are your thing, I've got a great lid."

Even in the dark, his eyes sparkled.

"And miss seeing you in your chef's hat? Not a chance."

"So tell me about this cowboy," Joe said.

I slowly exhaled and contemplated how I was going to present my story idea.

"What? Was this guy a creep?" The concern in his voice made me smile.

"No, I just … I may have a really good feature." I waited for Joe to say something, and when he didn't, I did. "Or it could be a sidebar to Kelly's piece."

A sidebar was nothing more than a few hundred words placed in a text box beside the main article in the newspaper. It was secondary, with no promise of a byline, and I knew it, but it no longer mattered where I appeared in the paper if I could write Frank's story.

"What's the angle?" My Thanksgiving date left and my editor appeared.

"One of the first homesteads on Casper Mountain was lost on Thanksgiving," I said, verbally drafting the story's lead. *He's so easy to talk to.*

"Was lost in the Thanksgiving Day fire," Joe said, already editing my copy. He reached behind him for a laptop. "Keep going."

"Um … " I grabbed my notebook and tilted it toward the window for light, but the moon was hidden behind dark, angry clouds. I activated the flashlight on my cell phone and shined it on my notes.

Joe's laptop screen glowed in the cab of his truck. "One of the first homesteads on Casper Mountain was lost in the Thanksgiving Day fire," he repeated as he typed.

I glanced at his fingers pecking the keys. "Uh, do you want me to do that?"

"No, I've got it. Let's keep going."

"Okay," I said and felt my heart skip a beat. *Yeah, let's do this.* "The home of the late Dr. Bob and Louise Outterland perished despite their grandson's valiant efforts to save it."

Joe's fingers feverishly worked the keys in spite of his henpecking approach. He looked up at me. "You verified this?"

"Yup." I smiled proudly in the dark. "With Chief Gambino."

"Good job. What else do you have?"

"Frank Outterland spent his Thanksgiving pouring buckets of water on the roof of his grandparents' homestead, echoing actions his grandfather had taken decades earlier in the fire of … " I snapped my fingers. "I don't know the exact date of that fire. I haven't verified it."

Joe held up his index finger while he scrolled through his computer. "1944. Kelly dug that up earlier."

"Oh, good," I said flatly. "Okay, so in the fire of 1944. A fire that was also started by a lightning storm. However, low humidity and gusty winds prevented the younger Outterland from saving his family's homestead when he had to evacuate the area."

"And the other cabin? Who did it belong to?"

"The other cabin was home to the Outterlands' son, Robert Jr., and his wife, Mary."

I worked through my notes page by page and dictated the story to Joe. The telegram, the Bible, the flag, and all that was in the fire. I poured every emotion I had left into this story because it was no longer my story—it was Frank's.

"How are you going to end this?" he asked with his head pointed toward his laptop.

I drew a deep breath that burned my lungs. Smoke filled the mountain with a fog-like thickness that weaved its way between trees, cars, and people, creating zero visibility.

I exhaled. "We need an early Christmas miracle," I said under my breath.

"What was that?" He leaned toward me.

I shrugged. "Something the chief said."

"What exactly did he say?"

I turned back to my notes. "I don't think I wrote it down. He said it as he was leaving."

"Close your eyes," Joe said.

"Huh?"

"Close your eyes and quiet your mind. Shut everything out."

It was well into the evening and I was tired, so complying wasn't difficult.

A few seconds passed and Joe spoke quietly. "Before the chief left, what did he say?"

"Unless we have an early Christmas miracle, we're going to lose the mountain. This fire isn't going to be contained any time soon." The chief's words flowed out of me verbatim as I heard Joe strike the keyboard.

He leaned over and kissed me quick and hard on the cheek. "Janey, that's brilliant."

"Is that the ending?" I asked.

"Not all stories begin simply or end neatly. *This* was one of those stories. It'll make readers follow us online, grab the next day's paper, and monitor our website."

"Huh."

Joe titled his laptop toward the dashboard. "Now to get a signal and email our front-page centerpiece."

"What?" My voice rose in octaves.

"They're going to have to re-plate the presses, but this is a great, great piece."

"I'm going to be on the front page?"

"Janey, your story *is* the front page."

Chapter 15

Dazed, I sat in Joe's truck while he initiated an Internet connection. I glanced at my cell phone. I had one bar of service. I quickly texted Kris.

> I made the front page! It doesn't seem right

I re-read the glowing screen, with my thumb hovering over the "send" key. Instead I hit "cancel" and the message disappeared. "Doesn't seem right."

"What's that?" Joe asked as his finger scrolled the mouse pad on his laptop.

"I *finally* landed a front-page story, but … " I looked out the passenger side window. Our breath had fogged the windows. I rubbed the sleeve of my sweater against the glass and saw a man in the distance holding a woman, comforting her. "So much was lost tonight."

"Got it!" Joe's voice made me turn toward him. "Come on, keep going." He leaned toward the laptop. A blue transmission line slowly inched across the screen. "Just a little more, baby." Joe clenched his fist and held it midair. "Come on, just a little more." When the blue line completed its course, he pumped his fist in the air and hit the ceiling of his truck. "Yes! We made it!" He leaned back and a look of relief crossed his face. "That was tight, but we made it just in time."

He glanced at me. I smiled softly.

"What were you saying? Something about lost?"

I shrugged. "It's nothing."

"No, it wasn't. What's up?"

Again, I turned my attention to the side window. "Look at that couple. Did they lose their home tonight? Do they even have a car? It just doesn't seem fair."

Joe didn't say anything. He turned the key in the truck's ignition and pressed a button on his car stereo. The opening chords of a guitar filled the cab with a melancholy melody.

"I'll be home for Christmas." The soft velvety voice of Bing Crosby resonated between us. "You can count on me."

My chest swelled with emotion. "I don't think this is helping." I looked for the couple, but they had disappeared into the night.

Joe inched beside me and sang, "Snow and mistletoe and presents by the tree."

I closed my eyes. His breath was hot in my ear, his lips grazed my neck. "Janey, you did a great job tonight. You told a story that will open readers' hearts to the reality of this fire. You made it real."

I nodded and felt a tear roll down my cheek. "I just thought it would be different." His hand gently wiped my cheek.

"You should be proud of your work."

I opened my eyes and stared at him while Bing Crosby crooned, "I'll be home for Christmas, if only in my dreams."

Joe softly kissed me. His lips caressed mine and held me. The local radio announcer's voice came up softly.

"That song is going out to Sally Owen from Tom, who's on Casper Mountain fighting the Thanksgiving Day fire. Our prayers are with all the firefighters tonight, many who missed Thanksgiving with their family to help other families. Clancy's Bar downtown has set up a food command center for those families displaced by tonight's fire. This next song's going out to all the men and women who need a little pick-me-up. Remember the code of the West, where we take pride in our work. This fire doesn't know what it's up against."

The twinkling sound of keys on a xylophone sparked a smiled on my face.

"I … don't want a lot for Christmas," Mariah Carey's sultry voice slowly sung the opening lyric to one of the best holiday songs ever.

"She's amazing." I turned up the volume.

Joe grinned. "She is saucy," he said above Mariah's high-reaching pitch.

He began to tap the dashboard to the beat of the song. I joined him. We drummed the dashboard and sang.

"Oh, I won't ask for much this Christmas."

"Only that we need snow," Joe changed the lyrics.

"Ohhhh, yeah!" I sang very off-key.

Mariah Carey's voice sang. "All I want for Christmas is you."

Joe pointed his finger toward me. "Make my wish come true, all I want for Christmas is you. You. You. You."

His over-the-top singing lifted my spirits. I laughed so hard I couldn't catch my breath.

Joe pulled me toward him and pushed hair off my face. His passion was contagious. For a moment, I forgot about the fire. He covered my mouth with his, and I lost myself in him.

"Baby, all I want for Christmas is you, you, you … "

• • •

The drive down the mountain was subdued. I glanced at the clock on the dash. It was past midnight. *I made it through my first Thanksgiving without my kids.*

"When do you have to get back home?" His gaze flicked to mine and then just as quickly turned back to the winding road.

"Tonight. I mean, later tonight, like by seven or eight. So I'll have to leave … by two in the afternoon to make it to Jackson in time."

"You can't stay longer?"

I hadn't had a man ask me to stay longer in forever. I found it hard to speak with my heart lodged in my throat.

Again, he briefly made eye contact with me.

"I wish I could," I said and pinched my nose to stop it from running. My eyes already brimmed with tears. *How can I be sad to leave someone I barely know?*

But I already knew the answer. I did know Joe, maybe not in the same familiar way that Kelly knew him, but there was a connection between us.

"You'll be back," he stated rather than asked. "On Christmas." He reached in the dark for my hand.

"I can't imagine being anywhere else," I said as I found his hand and held it tightly.

Chapter 16

We barely made it in the door of his home when, fully clothed, we collapsed together on his couch. We spooned and he held me all night and well into the morning. Our bodies formed perfectly against each other. We just fit.

A winter's sun shone across my face. I squinted until my vision came into focus. When it did, the first thing I saw was Joe's Christmas tree perched on the windowsill.

That tree might truly be the last relic from the mountain. *Oh, Joe.*

I held on to his arm around me and he pulled me tighter into him. *I don't want to go.* It felt so good, so natural, so right to be in his arms.

My cell phone buzzed in my back pocket.

"Is that your phone or does your butt always vibrate? Which is kind of hot." The sexy allure of his voice in my ear made leaving him that much more difficult.

I turned my head. His lips found me and his arms held me. His hand inched up my back and into my hair. He released my ponytail and curls slowly unraveled. He gently massaged my head and my curls sprung back into shape, full locks that brushed his skin and intensified his kisses. Cocooned in the passion of his embrace, I didn't hear his son enter the front room.

Sam cleared his throat. "Dad?"

Joe kissed me once more before he looked over my shoulder.

"The paper's on the house phone. They've called twice now, but I didn't want to wake you."

Joe leaned his forehead against me and spoke into my back. "Thanks, Sammy. Tell them I'll call back in a few minutes, okay?"

"Got it," Sam said.

My phone vibrated again.

"Looks like they found us," Joe said.

"The only person who knows where I am is my friend Kris."

Joe sat up "Don't be so sure."

"Huh?"

"Janey, your story was the front-page centerpiece in the statewide newspaper. If people didn't know your work before this, they will now. And if your ex is the jealous type, this will definitely get his attention."

"I don't think Mark knows how to read." I giggled.

Joe gently bit me on the shoulder. "He may not read the paper, but word spreads fast in small towns."

I shrugged. "So I was in Casper. We're divorced and he's remarried."

"Just be prepared. This kind of story will generate a lot of interest."

"Is this my editor talking or my Thanksgiving dinner host?"

He kissed my neck. "Both."

• • •

I stood beside my bug with the driver's side door open.

Joe pressed me against the door. "Stay another night."

"I wish I could."

"Do you need a note from your editor? Because I can arrange that."

I slowly shook my head and grinned.

"So ... " His sky-blue eyes locked in on me. This man seriously dripped with sex appeal. "Did you know there are only twenty-eight days left until Christmas?"

My body temperature spiked. "I did not know that."

"I thought maybe Sam and I would make one of those construction-paper chains."

I started to laugh.

"I'm serious. You know, the kind where you alternate between red and green paper links and each day you tear one off."

"I am all too familiar with construction paper crafts," I said.

"Then you should make one with John and Jessica. I bet they'd love doing that with their mom."

I nodded.

"So it's a deal?" he said.

I looked at him quizzically.

"When we both reach the last link in our chain, we'll be together again."

My stomach tightened. *Don't cry.* I felt my chest begin to shake with emotion. *Keep it together.* I couldn't answer. *Don't make me chose between you and my career. I've done that before and it doesn't work.*

"Janey." For the first time I saw worry cross his face. "Just say yes." He was strong enough for both of us.

Maybe I could have both. While I wanted to answer with what I hoped was possible, I answered with what I knew would protect me.

"I'll think about it."

Chapter 17

By the time I passed the elk refuge that welcomed me into Jackson's city limits, I had snuck glances at the front page of the paper throughout the drive home. My byline was front and center, above the fold—where a journalist lives and breathes. Even in black and white and Times New Roman font, it seemed surreal.

What wasn't surreal was the number of email messages that started to pour in once I was back into cell range. My phone chimed with a very full email inbox. I glanced at the screen and spotted Joe's name. My heart skipped a beat. I pulled over to the side of the road to read his message,

"Need you to call Chief Gambino for follow-up interview. He's expecting your call. I think you'll like the update. File copy by midnight—I'll be waiting. And congrats, Janey, you really hit a home run."

Midnight? Tonight? It was nearing eight and I still had to pick up my kids, get home, unpack, interview the fire chief, and write a story. *Impossible.*

I turned on the radio just as I was pulling up to my old house. There wasn't any update about the fire on the local station. *This is ridiculous.* And so were the outfits my ex-husband had chosen for our twin first graders.

They looked like Hansel and Gretel. At first glance, Jessica's brown corduroy jumper wasn't so bad. It was the white shirt with puffy sleeves and wraparound apron that clearly had to go. John was in brown overalls, suspenders, and a white shirt. All that was missing was a gingerbread house and an evil witch.

But what really made the fairy tale picture complete was when their new stepmom appeared on the front porch dressed to match my children. *Oh great, she's young enough to be dressing like seven-year-olds.*

"Thanks for being such good sports when we took our family Christmas photo," she said loud enough for my benefit.

Seriously?

"See you two next weekend," she said, before ducking back into my old house.

My fairy tale-clad children rushed down the driveway to greet me. I held out my arms and their little bodies crashed into me.

"Oh, my babies." The tops of their heads smelled like baby shampoo. "I missed you."

"Mommy! Did you bring us presents?" Jessica asked.

"Why would I have presents?"

"Because you were in Casper!"

I've been told I don't have a poker face, but shock is a hard emotion to mask.

"Nice front-page story, Turner." Mark's usual smugness surfaced and my usual forced air of solemnity followed.

"Thanks." I tussled Jessica's curly hair and fought the smile that was forming on my lips. *Front and center, baby.*

"Hey, do you have a second?" Mark's normally annoying voice was tentative.

"Yeah, let me get the kids in the car—it's heated and it'll keep them warm." They were sandwiched on either side of me. "Okay, kiddos, you have all your things?"

My towheaded boy and girl nodded in unison. I bit the inside of my cheek to stop from laughing. They looked like they were ready to serve beer at Oktoberfest. And Momma could use a beer just about now.

After buckling them into their car seats in the back of my bug, all I wanted was a little Fahrvergnügen, but instead I had to deal with my ex-husband. "What's up?"

"I really meant it about the story. It was a good piece," he said.

"Thank you." *So what is this really about?*

"Thanksgiving Day fire—that's not something that happens every day. And in Casper, no less."

I nodded.

"So do you have a new reporting job in Casper?" His voice piqued with interest.

And there it is. I spoke through gritted teeth. "Nope." *Not yet.*

"Oh." A look of disappointment shot across his face.

"Why?"

"Well, the airlines are looking to relocate a few of us to Cheyenne to work out of that airport hub. And I was thinking if you were working in Casper, it's only two hours from Cheyenne versus—"

"A seven hour drive from Jackson," I cut him off.

He nodded solemnly. "Yeah."

"Are they relocating you?"

He shrugged. "Right now it's kind of open, but … "

I had been the wife of an airline executive for a decade. I knew how it worked. Relocations always began with the illusion that the executive had the choice. It's how we ended up moving from Los Angeles to Jackson.

"Anyway, I thought if you had been reassigned to Casper, it'd be a real win-win." He tucked his hands into his pants pockets. "Well, I'll let you get the kids home. Congrats on the front page."

"Thanks." I walked to the car, the thought of relocating to Casper buzzing in my head. *Is that possible? Would there be a reporting job available?*

These thoughts dominated my attention as I drove toward the nearest convenience store. A bright red, coin-operated *Wyoming Frontier* newspaper rack was parked next to the trash can. If this was my one crack at a front-page story, I was going to pick up a few extra copies. I fished through my ashtray for every available quarter and kept the car running with heat blaring on John and Jessica while I ran to the machine.

Each time I dropped three quarters into the machine, pulled back the angled lid, and grabbed a paper, a new one popped forward. And each time my name was beneath the headline. My stomach did a little jig. It was better than a slot machine because the payoff was instant. Within minutes, I was back in the car with four new papers and an empty ashtray, and on the phone with Kris.

"Did you see the front page?"

Her throaty laughed followed. "I wondered when you were going to call me."

"Check me out." Adrenaline coursed through my veins. I held a crisp copy of the paper and pointed to my byline. "Hey, kiddos, whose name is that?"

"Mommy's!" I heard in duplicate.

"I'm just … oh, Kris, this is *everything* I've ever wanted. It's like I'm a *real* journalist."

Kris chuckled. "Janey, you are a journalist. The only person who doesn't believe that is you."

I placed the stack of papers on the passenger seat and stared at them.

"I can't tell you how proud I am of you," Kris said. "You've always been so willing to go the extra mile, and it's paying off. It's a fantastic story and a great photo. It gave me chills to see your name on the front page."

"Thank you," I said, my voice tender with emotion. "Joe wants me to interview the chief again and write a story—by tonight."

"Then get off the phone, get those sweet darlings to bed, and get cracking." Kris was a math teacher and nothing if not pragmatic. "And I'm here if you need me. I'll be grading a statistics assignment tonight so I'll be up. And don't even think you're going to get out of telling me all the other details about your dinner and your night."

I felt my cheeks burn with embarrassment. "What other details?"

Our laughter once again fused over the phone.

Chapter 18

The countdown to Christmas began early for Casper when a DC-10 delivered good news to the mountain community.

I leaned back on the couch in my living room. *What would Joe say about my lead?* I had been home less than three hours and already I missed his smell, his cooking, and most of all, his stenographer skills. I'd never dictated a story to someone. Even when I was in L.A., I'd text copy back to the office if I didn't have access to a computer—anything to avoid dealing with an editor. But Joe was different from the editors I had been assigned there. *What makes him so different?* I drummed my fingers on the keyboard and answered my own question. *He was a reporter before he was an editor.* Joe understood the process. I turned back to the story he'd assigned and kept writing.

Casper Mountain was drenched by a DC-10 fire bomber jet that dumped thousands of gallons of water on the middle of the fire, bringing the burn under containment. A Thanksgiving Day lightning strike ignited several fires on the mountain that devoured two cabin homes and forced the evacuation of 300 residents. Fire crews worked tirelessly throughout the night to combat flames on the steep terrain.

I glanced at my notes from my phone conversation with Chief Gambino, who was quick to remind me that I had promised he'd never hear from me again. I feigned an apology, but I don't think the chief bought it any more than I did. Joe was right. My story had picked up momentum. The paper tweeted it, I retweeted it, and so did thousands of Wyoming residents. It was going viral along with the picture I had taken of Frank and the chief, who liked the publicity for his department as much as I liked getting my name back out there. As my ex would say, it was a win-win. I reviewed my interview notes.

In total, the fire burned more than six square miles and a total of a hundred acres, up seventy acres from Thanksgiving night. More than 450 fire personnel from throughout the state were on the scene with aerial reinforcements that brought the fire into containment.

"Once the wind diminished, we started to really gain ground on the fire," Chief Charlie Gambino said.

My transition leading up the chief's next quote flowed from my fingers and appeared on the screen of my laptop.

The early Christmas miracle Chief Gambino hoped for appeared when snow fell from the skies.

I wish I had been there.

"I think the entire Cowboy State read that story about Frank Outterland losing his homestead and prayed for a miracle," Gambino said.

I paused. Emotions caught in my throat. *Joe was right. My story made a difference.* It felt odd to write a story about my cover article and the snowfall that I missed when I drove out of town, but Joe seemed to think I was the journalist for the job. And after seeing the front page, I had come to trust him in a way I hadn't imagined possible. *You gotta love a man who shows what's in his heart and doesn't just say it.*

I quickly concluded the piece.

While the fire is now contained, firefighters will continue to monitor the mountain for hot spots.

I hit the "save" button and opened my email. I typed the letter "J" and Joe's name surfaced. My stomach stirred with excitement, but my mind quickly assumed control. *Keep it professional. This is your career.* I attached my file to the new message and briefly wrote,

> Joe,
> Hope this is what you had in mind. Please advise if it requires editing or any adjustment.
> Thanks!
> Janey

I sat back and stared at the screen. The exclamation mark seemed to lighten the mood without overdoing it. I clicked "send" and headed toward a hot bath.

Two hours later, I lay in bed and stared at the alarm clock on my nightstand. Twelve o'clock flashed in red neon. I checked my phone. No missed calls or emails. I hugged my pillow, and without any warning, tears fell. Was this about Mark moving? Oh my hell. Why would that make me cry? Or was it over Joe not calling? I could've called him. I put my spinning thoughts to a halt and texted Kris.

> Joe hasn't called. Or emailed. And Mark may be moving to Cheyenne.

Her reply made sense:

> Long day. Mark just trying to steal your thunder & Joe's probably crashed. U need sleep. Give it 24 hrs.

Chapter 19

My eyes were adjusting to the morning light when his email came into view.

> Janey—
> Thought we'd keep the momentum going on the fundraising efforts to rebuild the Outterland family homestead. Interview Frank for his reaction and any other Outterland you can wrangle.
> Thanks!
> Joe

I tossed my smartphone back onto the bed and pulled the covers up around me. I had finally upgraded my phone, and now I wish I hadn't. Before my smartphone, I had time to wake up, turn on my computer while I poured a cup of coffee, and then see what sterile email my Thanksgiving host had sent. Now when I woke up, Joe's professional, to-the-point, perfectly normal editor-assigning-reporter emails surfaced instantaneously. There was no amount of caffeine to offset the tension that this standoff, which we had both seemingly entered, created. A week had passed and neither of us was broaching the topic of "that night." While nothing happened, it remained stuck in limbo and so did my feelings.

"Maybe he's playing me." I waved my hand to clear the mushy thought that found its way out of my mouth. It didn't help. All I knew was that Joe had awakened in me something I had let go dormant: my heart. And I didn't know how to make it hibernate again any more than I knew how to tell him how I felt. Or worse, ask about a possible reporting job in Casper.

"What the hell?" I spoke into the phone before Kris even had a chance to say hello. "Why couldn't I have found the postman attractive? Ray's a good guy. Married, but at least I'd see him every day. And this unrequited love would eventually lessen because I'd realize Ray is just not my guy. But *not* seeing Joe and getting work emails from him is awful because it keeps me wondering."

"And you're wondering about what, Miss Janey?"

I shrugged. "Whether it was real. The connection we had. Or did my love of the story eclipse our moment?"

"Would you have done anything differently?"

"No."

"Then that's your answer. You and Joe had a fun Thanksgiving dinner that led to a fantastic front-page article. End of story. If there was anything else, one of you would have made more of an effort."

I pressed back against the pillow, absorbing the unexpected blow her words brought. "Ouch."

"If you don't like how that sounds, then do something different."

"Why are you so logical? Don't you have any demons? Conflicting emotions?"

Startled laughter seeped through the phone. "Oh, Miss Janey, you know I have past demons. I just don't let them rule my future."

"You're too healthy to be my friend."

"Listen, I feel somewhat responsible for the situation you're in."

If Kris were in my bedroom with me, I know I'd be giving her a bewildered look because I couldn't imagine how she was responsible for any of this. "And you feel this way, why?"

"I'm the one who suggested you invite yourself to Thanksgiving dinner, and while you didn't exactly invite yourself to Joe's, you ended up there just the same. And professionally, it turned out to be great, but personally, I feel bad that it's left you feeling this way."

I stared at the ceiling fan above me that slowly rotated to allow the heat to circulate in my room. "Kris, this isn't on you. You're right. If I want things to be different, I should do something different. I'm just not sure what to do. Then there's the whole issue of asking about a reporting job." I exhaled and added more hot air to the room. "It'd be better if I let this thing die and maintained a professional relationship with him versus telling him how I feel and risk losing both my job and him."

"How *do* you feel about him?"

My body responded with a swift wave of emotions that both ached to see and kiss Joe and hurt since neither of us were doing anything to make that happen. "I like him."

"Then don't settle for one or the other. Get the job and then get Joe."

For the first time since I left Casper, I felt like my feet were firmly planted on solid ground. "Yeah, I can do that. Job. Then Joe."

"So what are you going to do?"

A sudden gust of breath filled me as a shot of adrenaline surged through my veins. "It's something I thought up on the mountain. Let me write it and you'll be the first to read it. No"—I shook my head and grinned widely—"Joe will."

Chapter 20

Five Fun Ways to Meet Your Someone Special This Holiday Season

I typed the headline and then leaned back against the barstool. *Okay it's not a craft column, but it's the next best thing. Besides, there are only so many crafts you can make out of pinecones.* Sadly, I knew this because I had checked online. And pinecones wouldn't hold a reader's interest, but how to have a happily after ever this holiday season? Oh, yeah. It was brilliant. I grabbed my coffee cup and took a big gulp. It was bitter, but it'd do the trick. I could practically feel the caffeine shoot through me.

From taking a chance and accepting a blind dinner date to the old, but reliable, accidentally stepping under the mistletoe move, the holidays are a great time to create a spark.

My fingers danced across the keyboard. *I may have to rework the lead, but I'm on to something.* I hit the number key function and "1" appeared indented on the page.

1. Dashing through the snow? Hop on a sled, get in a sleigh, and see where the road takes you. If you end up at an old friend's house—all the better. And if you're the house where an old acquaintance shows up, open the door. Let the spirit of the season be welcoming to all.

2. O Christmas Tree, O Christmas Tree. It doesn't have to be big and bright to make someone's holiday wish come true. And this season, there are plenty of trees that need a good home. Go see Chief Gambino and ask for a little potted pine. For $5 you can help raise funds for the Outterland homestead. Then find that someone special

to help decorate the tree. After the holidays, you can make a date to plant the tree on Casper Mountain.

3. Here comes Santa Claus! And he needs a few helpers. Volunteer at the food bank, offer to collect new gifts for the toy drive, or simply help out your neighbor. Santa's watching and you never know who you may meet when you're doing good deeds!

4. Home alone for the holidays? Offer to cover a colleague's shift at work. You won't be alone and you can spread your cheer all day long. You may even be amazed to find out who else is working the holiday beside you.

I worked through my list and concluded with my personal favorite.

5. It's beginning to look a lot like Christmas. So turn on the oven and start baking some holiday treats. What better way to someone's heart than through a gift basket of goodies? Be safe and avoid anything with nuts.

I seriously felt I was on fire by the time I spellchecked and composed my email to Joe.

Joe—

Two pieces attached. First, the feature on the Outterland fundraising efforts. Second, a column for our weekend readership that ties back into one of the fundraising efforts for the new Outterland homestead. I noticed there was a weekend slot open for a columnist, and I thought I'd try my hand at column writing. What do you think?

When you get the chance, I'd like to talk to you about expanding my reporting duties to include Casper.

Thanks!

Janey

I attached the two files and scrolled my finger over the touchpad until the cursor hovered over "send." I pressed down and clicked it into the clouds. I wasn't going to overthink it or obsess. I was going after what I wanted: the job, then Joe.

Chapter 21

The beauty about the newspaper industry was that when a writer nailed a piece and truly hit the mark, a preview to the story was posted immediately online and the full story was published in the print edition. It was a twofer. But in my case, only one of my stories was teased and then released in print.

"It didn't work." My voice was as flat as my enthusiasm.

"Oh, Janey. I'm sorry."

"Yeah, Joe emailed me back. Should I read it to you?" I didn't wait for her to reply.

> Janey,
> Cute idea for a column. Let me give it some thought. Thanks for the follow-up on the Outterland fundraising efforts. Solid reporting. We'll touch base on the possibility of expanding your reporting area.
> Thanks!
> Joe

"He thought the column was 'cute.' Cute." I shook my head.

"Janey, that doesn't sound so bad."

"Cute? Cute is the kiss of death in my industry. Journalists or columnists don't write cute, they write, well, what he said about my feature—solid. Not cute. Eh, it doesn't matter now." I shrugged. "He didn't even mention a date to run my cute column so I guess … " I massaged my forehead. "What the hell was I thinking?"

"That you could woo him with your writing?"

I frowned. "Yeah, that usually works. I thought maybe he'd see that I was multitalented, offer me the columnist position, expand my reporting base, and then ask if I was coming for Christmas."

"You really aimed for the fence." Kris's daughters played softball. Her analogies tended to relate back to sports.

I nodded. "Yup, but instead of hitting the fence, I struck out." I felt nauseous. "I give up. It's obviously not meant to be. He's my editor. We shared Thanksgiving dinner and that's all there was to it."

"Are you sure he hasn't called you?"

"He has my cell number."

"But when you recently upgraded you switched providers and they gave you a new number."

"That's true, but he still has my home landline number and my email. If he wanted to reach me, he could." I closed my laptop and pushed away from the kitchen counter. "The sooner I let go of this, the better."

Chapter 22

After two more weeks of nothing but short, curt work emails from Joe, sleep still didn't come easy. My nights were restless with the reality that he wasn't going to reach out to me beyond his role as editor. And I had already made the first move, at least toward bridging the distance between us by having a Casper-based job. *I'm not going to be the clingy Thanksgiving guest from hell.* Christmas break had started and now each morning my twins came into my room, gently touched my face, and kissed my forehead.

"What time is it?" I fumbled for my phone and woke up the screen. When it came to life, I felt mine take a dive. No new email messages from work. "Do we have school?" John asked.

I shook my head. "No, sir, you do not."

"What about me?" Jessica asked.

I choked back a chuckle. "No, baby girl, no school for you either."

"What are we going to do?" they asked.

I pulled back the covers and patted the mattress. "Come join me."

My twins piled in and we burrowed beneath my fluffy down comforter.

"It's snowing," John said. "And Daddy said that means Santa's reindeers are practicing for their big flight on Christmas Eve."

"I bet Rudolph is leading them through the snow *right* now," I said.

"Do you still believe in Santa?" Jessica asked.

"Of course. Don't you?"

She shrugged. "I dunno. I heard Suzie Clark tell her little brother, Stephen, that Santa wasn't coming to their house this year."

I knew the Clarks were in the middle of a divorce, but I didn't know any of the details. Nor did I need to know them.

"I have an idea," I said. "Have you ever heard of a Secret Santa?"

My first graders shook their heads.

"Well, sometimes, Santa gets super busy during this time of the year and he needs a little help. So he asks certain families to help out other families by dropping off presents, food, and stockings ... " *What am I about to get myself into in my need to keep my emotions under control? It's one thing to write about being one of Santa's helpers, it's an entirely different thing to do it.* But the surprised looks on my twins' faces told me I was on the right path. "Okay, so we have to do this in secret. No one can know."

"Oh, because we're helping Santa?" Jessica's large, brown eyes searched mine for an answer.

"That's right," I said, gently poking her in the belly. "You're so smart."

My daughter lit up in a smile. "Another day with Mommy!" she said.

And another day without Joe.

Chapter 23

Nearly all the green and red construction paper links on my children's countdown-to-Christmas chain were gone. The twins and I had made the chain the day after I got home from Casper. Now, any time I looked it, I thought of Joe. Our communication had boiled down to a weekly email that consisted of a few words about my story assignments and my minimal reply.

I grabbed a potholder from the kitchen drawer and slipped my hand inside.

The subtle smell of vanilla and the richness of molasses perked my senses and awakened my hunger. I could almost taste the air. *Christmas.*

I snuck a peek through the oven window. The gingerbread men puffed in the center. The cut-out cookies looked more like a lineup of potbellied cowboys.

I carefully opened the oven. The last batch of cookies rose very fast and high and then fell as soon as I placed the tray on the top of the oven. I was determined that at least one of my relationships with a man would work out this holiday season—even if he was made of dough.

Heat encircled my arm as I reached for the cookie sheet. I was carefully backing up with the tray of cookies in one hand when John ran into the kitchen.

"Mommy, we got a package!" My first grader darted behind me and bumped my elbow. I lost hold of the cookie sheet.

Gingerbread scattered into the air as men toppled around me. I covered my head, but a cookie still dinged me. The aluminum cookie sheet fell like a quarter on a toss. It teetered, clanged, and reverberated against the tiled kitchen floor. I jumped, but the corner of the hot tray nicked my ankle. I grabbed my burnt heel and hopped in place. This caused my "Ho! Ho! Ho!" embossed sweatshirt to rise off my midriff. The soft skin singed against the open oven door when I accidentally bounced into it.

"Help." I bumped the oven shut with my hip.

"Uh-oh." John's brown eyes opened wide. "Did I do that?" His voice was small and unassuming.

I shook my head. "It was an accident. I'm trying to … " *Keep my mind off missing my editor.* "Mommy's doing too much and making a mess." I ran a paper towel beneath the cold water tap in the kitchen sink and applied it to my heel. "But running in the house probably isn't a good idea."

John gently patted my arm. "I'm sorry you're so klutzy that you ran into me."

I couldn't help but laugh and then slid another tray of gingerbread men into the oven.

"Can we open the box?" Jessica walked into the kitchen with a pair of scissors in her hand.

"It's probably another Christmas present," I said, applying the wet towel to my burnt skin. "Why don't you put it under the tree?

"So we can't open it?" she said, putting the scissors down on the kitchen table.

"Who is it from?" I asked.

My daughter ran into the foyer of our townhouse. I heard her carefully sounding out the words. "Um… it's from Joe … R-gen-tee."

"Joe Argenti?" I dropped the wet towel and dashed past my son toward the front room.

A small box wrapped in brown paper was addressed to me with Joe's home address as the return. I carefully took the box and sat down on the couch, which was now in front of our Christmas tree. The star on the top of the tree glistened with hope.

"Who is Joe R-gen-tee?" Jessica asked, sitting beside me.

"No one." I looked at the box and wanted to hurl it across the room.

"Why did he send you a box?"

I shrugged. "I probably left something behind on Thanksgiving," I said without any care what my twins would report back to their father.

"Is he your friend?" John asked, sidling up beside me on the couch.

"I thought he was. But ... " My twins clung to my every word.

"Maybe it's from Santa!" My daughter's voice grew with excitement. "Like the man on the phone talked about."

I practically bolted off the couch. "Jess, what man? What are you talking about?"

"I told you, you shouldn't have picked up the phone. You're in trouble," John said.

I held up my hands. "No one's in trouble. I just need to know what man. Was there a man in the house?" My adrenaline kicked into overdrive. I looked toward the hall closet where I kept a baseball bat.

"No, he was on the phone."

I grabbed my cell phone out of my back jeans pocket. "Mommy's new phone?"

She shook her blonde curls. "No, he was on the house phone."

I darted toward the kitchen. I grabbed the portable landline and hit the "missed calls" feature, but no numbers popped up. "Jess, did you pick up the phone?" I yelled from the kitchen.

"Yes!"

I ran back to the front room with the portable house phone. "You picked up this phone?"

She nodded.

"And there was a man on it? Was it Grandpa? Or Uncle Mike?"

She shook her head. "Nope. He asked for my mommy."

"Oh, so maybe it was just a salesman?" Relief started to work its way through my body. "Did he say what he wanted?"

"Yeah, he said he wanted to eat your story."

"What?" I shook my head. "He wanted to eat it?"

Jessica slowly moved her head up and down. "He said he was your eater and he needed to talk to you about eating your story."

"Eater?" I scratched my mess of curls. "Eater." I paced the front room, tapping the portable phone against the palm of my hand. "Oh! Editor?" I turned toward Jessica. "Did he say he was my editor?"

"Yes! That's what I said—your eater."

I plopped down on the couch and thumbed through the stored list of phone numbers—both received and dialed. The *Wyoming Frontier*'s main switchboard number surfaced. The call came in two weeks ago. *Oh, no.* I frantically hit the number and heard the phone automatically dial it.

"Hi, Carmen, it's Janey. I'm trying to reach … " I paused. "I'm not really sure. My daughter picked up a call, but it was weeks ago, from an editor. I'm sure it was the night editor and whatever they needed passed … "

"Hey, Janey, it was probably from Joe."

"What? How can you be sure? It was two weeks ago." The desperation in my voice couldn't be hidden.

"Well, I think it was him." Her voice sounded as uncertain as my emotions. "Did you change your cell number?"

I nodded. "Yeah, I switched carriers so I could get a smartphone." *And be more hip like Kelly.*

"Can you email us your new number? All we have is your home phone, and I'm pretty sure it was Joe who wanted to talk to you."

"Really? Do you think it was Joe?" My voice contained way too much enthusiasm. I cleared my throat. "Um, could you connect me?"

Within seconds, I heard, "Newsroom, this is Joe Argenti."

My pulse quickened. "Hey."

"Janey?"

I nodded. "Yeah. I'm returning your call."

"Could you hold on for a second?" He didn't sound like himself.

My heart plummeted to the pit of my stomach. "Of course."

"Hello there." His voice was lower, and the sexy allure that I hadn't heard for more than three weeks filled my soul with a sound that had been missing from my life. "I had to go into the conference room."

My stomach stirred with excitement. "So, I missed a call?"

"Yeah, like two weeks ago. When I tried your cell, an automated voice told me your number had been disconnected. So I tried your home number and your daughter told me you were playing secret Santa with Suzie Clark's father. I figured you were busy so I didn't call back."

"What?" Panic gripped my voice. John and Jessica leaned toward me. "Um, hold on," I said into the phone and then placed it against my sweatshirt to muffle the sound. "Hey, this is Mommy's work. Can you give me a minute? Maybe you could make a list of things we still need to do before Christmas."

Jessica clapped her hands. "Yeah!"

John followed her off the couch.

"Sorry about that. I had little ears. Suzie Clark's father is going through a divorce. And I wasn't playing Santa with him or anyone, we were leaving gifts for their kids."

There was silence. I crossed my arms over my chest. *Fine. Whatever.*

"In your column you wrote about being Santa's helper. I figured that was what you were doing."

"So you haven't called or emailed beyond your editor duties because a seven-year-old told you that I was playing Santa's helper?" My tone was as snide as I intended.

"No, that's not why I didn't call back or email you. I'm a little more mature than that."

"Then why? Why haven't you reached out to me?" *Mr. Maturity.*

"Janey, when I asked you to come back for Christmas, you said you'd think about it."

My heart pounded and then plummeted to my stomach. *Oh. I never said yes.*

"It wasn't what I expected to hear." His voice was sharp and curt. He paused, and in that silence my chest ached. "It threw me," he said. "Janey, it really confused me."

"I was protecting myself," I said.

Joe's rich, hearty laughter suddenly filled my ear. "So was I. That's why I took a step back. I thought that's what you wanted."

I began to laugh. "No, well, yes. It's not easy. You're my editor."

"I thought we had separated that when you came to my house for dinner."

My throat was tight and my eyes began to mist. "I thought so, too, but you're still my editor. And I can't afford to lose my job if things go south. So I didn't say yes. I probably should've said yes but … " I placed my hand on my chest to stop it from hurting. "I didn't know. So instead I tried to woo you with my work and that column and … I'm not very good at this." *I'm an idiot.*

Again, his deep, masculine laughter echoed in my ear. "Janey, when you came back to my truck on Thanksgiving night with the front-page story of the decade, you wowed me."

"So I didn't need to write that column?"

He chuckled. "No, but it is going to run this weekend. Stan loved it. Thought you had a real talent for column writing."

I grinned. "So there's an upside to all of this."

Joe didn't say anything.

"My ex-husband's job is most likely relocating him to Cheyenne."

Joe still didn't utter a word.

"That's why I wanted to talk to you about expanding my reporting duties to include Casper ... well, actually, to be Casper."

"I got that email, and it wasn't something I thought should be discussed through an email exchange. I still don't."

"Okay."

"It's something we should discuss in the newsroom during our weekly assignment meetings."

"What?"

"Janey, the *Wyoming Frontier* needs good reporters like you. If you're willing to relocate to Casper, there's a desk and a reporting beat waiting for you."

"Really?"

"Yes, really."

I spun on the heels of my boots and raised my fist in the air. "Oh, my gosh!" I giggled.

"I miss hearing you laugh," he said.

"I miss you." It escaped my lips before I could take it back. I closed my eyes and held my breath.

"Well, that's originally why I had called." His tone began to shift. He didn't sound like my editor or my Thanksgiving host. "I'm glad you finally called me back." He was pensive and his mood changed.

"Joe, I never got the message. It was left with a seven-year-old."

"Understood. There's still something I wanted to talk to you about," he said.

"Fine." My body tightened, preparing for the blow. *I got the job, but I won't get the guy. I can't have both.*

"I called a few days after you left because I thought that twenty-eight, well, now it's three days, was just way too long a time."

Even though I had prepared myself, I still felt sucker-punched. The wind literally left my lungs. I murmured, "I understand."

"Well, that's why Sam and I were talking about taking a road trip to Jackson Hole."

"What?" *He wanted to see me.*

"We were trying to find a weekend when I wasn't the on-call editor and Sam didn't have a band performance, but … " He hesitated. "There never was a weekend where we were both available."

"Oh, that's okay. It's a long drive for just a weekend."

"Janey."

I closed my eyes and imagined his lips as he spoke.

"I want this to work," he said. Suddenly, the subtle change in his voice made sense. He was as uncertain about my feelings as I was about his.

"I've been waiting for you to call or email something more than an assignment," I said.

"It didn't seem like that's what you wanted. Your emails have been pretty flat and informative."

"Yeah, my BFF may have mentioned that. I just didn't want to cross a line professionally—it was awkward."

"Do you know how many times I've reached for the phone?" he asked.

"About as many times as I've checked mine to see if it was still working?"

We both laughed.

"So maybe you can update our records with your new cell phone number," he said, sounding very much like my editor. And then his voice softened. "That's boy code for 'I'd like to be able to call you when I'm not at work.'"

"Thanks for clearing that up for me." I smiled.

"No problem. I've been told I'm not always direct," he said with a chuckle. "Did you get the box I sent?"

I picked it up off the couch and held it. "It just arrived."

"Have you opened it?"

"No. I was afraid maybe I had left something behind in Casper."

"You did."

"Really? What?" I asked.

"Me."

Tears streamed down my face. "So what are you sending me?"

"Your way back."

"Hey, Joe!" I heard a male voice in the background.

"Oh, crap. Listen, we've got breaking news here today," he said. "Open the box."

The call disconnected. I held the phone against my chest and looked up at the star on the Christmas tree. *Thank you.*

"John? Jessica?" I called for my twins.

They ran down the hallway and into the front room.

"Can someone carefully get me the pair of scissors on the kitchen table?"

Jessica ran into the kitchen. She returned and handed me her craft scissors, and I slid the dull blade across the side of the box. I gently pulled on the cardboard until the lid opened. A velvety red stocking with "Janey" written in cursive and outlined in silver glitter was tucked inside.

"Oh, Mommy, that's pretty," Jessica said.

"It is, and I think he made this for me." I held up the stocking and the contents shifted toward the toe. I reached inside and pulled out three gift cards for gas, a movie, and pizza, a pack of gum, mints, candy canes, and a CD.

"I bet it's from your Secret Santa!" John said.

"Like what we did," Jessica said and then lowered her voice. "For the Clark family."

"It may be," I told my son and daughter.

A note was tucked inside.

Janey, use this to fill up on gas and treat your kids to dinner and a movie. The CD is for a long road trip. Have any planned? Thinking of you—Joe.

I grabbed the disk and looked for a playlist. Instead, the CD read in bold, black marker: "I'll Be Home For Christmas." My eyes brimmed with tears.

"Oh, Mommy, your Secret Santa loves you," John said.

I swallowed, but it didn't dislodge the lump in my throat.

"What are you going to give him?" Jessica asked.

I smelled my next batch of cookies burning.

"Dessert."

Chapter 24

Christmas Eve. The windowpanes in my master bedroom were frosted with snow. A candle slowly burned on my nightstand, releasing cinnamon into the air. I pulled the sleeve of my sweater over my hand and wiped the windowpane. Outside, the town of Jackson glowed from house lights and street lamps that seemed to say, "Merry Christmas."

My cell phone chimed with an incoming call. It was Kris. "How are you doing?"

I shrugged. "I just dropped off the kids." I swallowed. "I won't be able to see them run down the stairs to see what Santa left." I shook my head, but it didn't prevent tears from collecting in the corners of my eyes. "I hate this."

"So what are you going to do?" Kris was always my North Star.

"Get drunk on cooking vanilla?"

I loved it when I could make Kris burst into laughter. "Janey! You will not get drunk on vanilla. Don't you at least have brandy or something?"

"I'd rather drink vanilla; brandy is just plain nasty."

"Seriously. Why don't you come over and join me and Stephen and the girls? We're going to break out the board games and have a rousing time of Parcheesi."

Now I broke into laughter. "As fun as that does sound, and let me tell you, I *am* the queen of the Parcheesi board, this is your first Christmas with your new husband. I'm not going to crash the party. And aren't your girls going out caroling later with the high school youth group?"

"Yes, but … "

"Yeah, I know as soon as you see the taillights of their car pull away, you and Stephen will be playing hide the mistletoe."

I knew my best friend was blushing as she giggled. "We have all night to be together," she said. "It's only five thirty."

A layer of dark blue hung on the horizon, casting a sapphire tint on the Grand Tetons that rose high into the sky. Their peaks were covered by clouds. "It seems later," I said.

"Nah, that's just winter."

I glanced at my laptop. A red bleep moved across the map of the United States. "Santa's in New York. He's on his way toward us," I said. "I think."

"You really have no sense of direction, do you?"

"Nope. It's amazing I made it to Casper."

There was a moment of silence between us.

"You know what I'm thinking?" Kris said.

"That if I leave now I'll make it to Casper by midnight?"

"You'll be there at eleven thirty, with enough time to enjoy thirty minutes of Christmas Eve with Joe."

"He's not expecting me until tomorrow."

"Yeah, I see how that would present a problem because men *are* such sticklers about etiquette."

"Oh, har har."

"Why are we still on the phone? Shouldn't you be packing?"

I giggled. "I may have packed three days ago after I got off the phone with him."

"Drive safe and text me when you get there."

"This isn't stupid, right?" It was the same question I had posed to her while I drove on Thanksgiving.

"Janey, don't overthink this. Let your heart be your guide. What does your heart say—not your head, your heart?"

My chest rose and fell with emotion. "It's telling me that I *really* like this guy."

"So go play Santa."

"Ho, ho, ho." I blew out the candle on my nightstand while Kris laughed in my ear.

"And tell me *all* about it," she said.

"Merry Christmas!" I ended our call, walked to my closet, grabbed my overnight bag, and headed for my car.

Chapter 25

The CD that Joe burned for me filled my bug with every imaginable Christmas song, from Charlie Brown and the gang sweetly singing "Christmas Time is Here," which reminded me of my twins, to the singing duo of Zooey Deschanel and M. Ward belting out "Rockin' Around The Christmas Tree," which made me bounce in my seat.

I pulled into Casper's city limits as the last track played. Bing Crosby's silky voice brought back memories of Thanksgiving on the mountain.

"Christmas Eve will find me, where the love light gleams."

The Outterland exit beckoned me toward its highway turnoff. I flipped on my turn signal and followed the road as it dipped and rose, taking me to a plateau where I could see Casper Mountain in the distance. The fire had long been contained. Now, cleanup efforts to clear debris and harvest trees were in full swing.

I drove to Joe's house and parked on the street just outside his front window. My cell phone was on the passenger seat beside a tray of flat gingerbread men my children had heavily frosted. Red, green, and yellow iced gingerbread men smiled at me. Not a nut in the batch. I scrolled my contacts for Joe's number.

I hit "call" and nervously tapped my boot against the floor mat.

"Hey, what are you doing?" It always sounded like Joe was smiling when he spoke.

"What are *you* doing?"

"I'm getting ready to go to midnight service."

"Really?"

"Yeah, Sam's with his mom. And I was just thinking, imagining really, what it'd be like to go with you," he said. "Maybe next year? Then you'll be in town."

"What about this year?" My voice was barely above a whisper. "What about this Christmas Eve?"

"Oh, that would have been great. We could have gone to this all-night truck stop afterward and had breakfast," he said.

I got out of my car and stood on the sidewalk. The shades in his front room were open and his little mountain Christmas tree had a single strand of lights wrapped around it.

"Your Christmas tree looks amazing. It's so much bigger," I said.

"Yeah, Sam and I found some mini lights." Joe stopped talking. He appeared in his front window and peered out. He didn't have a poker face either. "You're here," he said.

"I used your present." My eyes began to brim. "Is it okay that I'm early?"

He disappeared from view and tears rolled down my cheeks. His front door opened and he rushed toward me. I practically dropped my phone. Joe caught it and pulled me toward him.

"You made it home for Christmas," he said. His blue eyes were majestic and held me as tightly as his embrace. "It's not just a dream."

I smiled and shook my head. "No dream. I'm real."

Joe wiped a tear from my face and tilted my chin toward him. His lips were warm and inviting. They made their way from my mouth, to my cheek, to my neck. He whispered softly in my ear, "Merry Christmas, Janey," as he pressed me even tighter against him. "And you know that's boy code for 'I love you.'"

I nodded against him. "Oh, Joe, I 'Merry Christmas' you, too."

A Sneak Peek from Crimson Romance (From *Christmas Clash* by Dana Volney)

Luke Carrigan crumpled the unwanted letter in his hand and swung open the glass door to the flower shop with the other. Silver chimes cheerily flickered above him, and if he could've turned around and karate chopped them down, he would've.

"I thought you were an Ellison." He walked toward the dark-haired woman behind the counter and spotted a red poinsettia. *Freaking Christmas.* "Can't you fix this?" The paper cracked as it hit the counter and dewy humidity filled his nose.

Candace paused, holding a white rose between her soft pink nails, and swiveled to face him. "Good morning to you, too." She may have suppressed an eye roll, but it still resonated in her voice.

He heard rustling behind her and caught a glimpse of red hair behind a very large green plant.

"Why am I getting a notice about the city taking my bar? Again?" He rested his hands on the cold granite. "Didn't you speak to them?" He censored his words in an attempt at civility since they weren't alone.

In one swift motion she swiped her chin-length black hair behind her ear. "Well, Luke, a *last name* doesn't fix anything." Her eyes met his.

The most annoying thing about Candace Ellison was her brilliant, piercing blue eyes. Her full, always-tainted-pink lips were a close second. They were alluring features that promised excitement and fulfillment, but in reality only provided an unfounded fantasy. Luke stepped back from the counter and folded his arms across his chest.

"So, you are going to be of no help?" He raised a brow.

"That's *not* what I said, now, is it? Calm yourself down." She entwined another rose in the overflowing green-and-gold-striped glass vase. "What are you doing up so early? Shouldn't you be sleeping something off?" A smile played on her generous lips as he grunted.

Ah, the crap he had to put up with to save the family pub was getting harder to swallow. Two years ago, the moment his dad's pen had lifted from the ownership transfer papers, Luke had felt the pressure. The weight worsened when his dad had looked at him, tension darkening his eyes, and said, "She's all yours now, my boy. Take care of her like the generations before you have." In other words, don't screw up what years and years of hard labor had produced, and if Luke did he'd never live down the disappointment.

"Hilarious." He turned to leave and mumbled under his breath, "Why do I bother?"

Snow crunched beneath his boots a few minutes later as he walked next door to his pub. Candace was an Ellison, which meant she would only do what was in *her* best interest—no matter the cause. She'd been that way since he could remember, and his memory on the subject was long. He'd never cared about her family name or their money, but Candace had seemed to and that rubbed him the wrong way. They'd known each other since kindergarten. Okay, *known* might be a strong word—more like despised. They were oil and water, fire and ice, Ralphie and his Red Ryder B.B. gun—any of those comparisons would do.

Not that he thought about their relationship a lot.

The sun was new in the blue sky, but did little to heat the air of the morning. He opened the heavy, dark oak door to his family's business, The Pub. Candace had been right about his hours, but he wasn't a drunken bartender anymore. The Pub wasn't some gig he waltzed in and out of because it was the family business. As third-generation Carrigan, the pub had been passed down to him. And losing it to the city under his watch wasn't going to happen.

If he would've gotten involved in the business district of Casper more and followed politics, like his dad had suggested, then maybe he could've prevented his business being put on the chopping block. As it was, besides his neighbors and the locals that drank at the bar, he had no special connections. Not of the powerful variety, anyway.

David Deehan looked up from cleaning bar glasses and Luke shook his head curtly once, kept walking straight into his office, and claimed his dilapidated green office chair. *Not sure why I thought she'd come through.* That was a lie—he'd assumed one call to the mayor or president of the city council from an upset Ellison would have fixed the problem that'd been building. There was no way Candace would've made that call if the proposed demolition had only affected him, but it didn't. Her flower shop was just as much in the damage zone as his pub, not to mention the five other businesses around them. He'd hoped her self-preservation instincts would've kicked in by now. He spun around in the chair and tapped his pen on his leg. *Think, man, think.* A soft knock beckoned from his open door. He stopped turning his chair to see Candace standing in his doorway.

Perhaps she'd grown a conscience in the last thirteen minutes and he was in line for a Christmas miracle.

"Yes?" He moved his left hand to the arm of the chair and shifted his body to the right.

"There's a town hall meeting tonight. Are you going?" She leaned against the door frame, emphasizing her black, long-sleeved shirt with its swirl of flowers and her shop's logo that was as vibrant as her arrangements. In jeans and no jacket, despite the chilly Wyoming winter, she looked good.

If only I could get women I actually liked to chase me down like this.

"Wouldn't miss it. *I'm* going to try to do something."

"And, what? You think I haven't?" She pursed her lips and narrowed her blazing blue eyes. "At least I had options to try."

"Options?"

One, maybe. She'd probably called Daddy or her brother, Blake. Though he shouldn't be so hard on Blake—that was the Ellison he probably should've called in the first place. Hindsight was always twenty-twenty.

"I can't wave a magic wand and change five minds. There are people to go through, schmooze. And the one who is heading up this little convention project is … not exactly a family friend."

"You mean to tell me the Ellisons don't own Casper?" He should've let up, but frustration fueled him.

"*No.* The Ellisons don't own Casper, or Wyoming for that matter. You're such a prick." She rolled her eyes, this time literally. "Without Jeffrey Dean pulling the plug on this motion, it'll go to a preliminary vote, then an actual vote. Maybe even tonight."

Luke smiled slowly, more out of contempt than humor. "Glad we've cleared that up. Now, if you'll excuse me, I'm thinking here."

Her subtle orange-vanilla scent made its way to him and he briefly forgot how to exhale. *How does a woman so irritating smell so delicious?* His eyes shifted to the Chamber of Commerce plaque on the hunter green wall beside her before he resumed breathing.

"I'd hate to interrupt *that* process." She rested her hand on the broad area of her hip. Luke let his gaze drift down to her fingertips, but only momentarily. He found her eyes again, and hers didn't seem to notice his stolen glance.

"What have you come up with?"

Her genuine tone caught his attention.

"Nothing yet." He willed himself to keep his face free of emotion. She'd most certainly use the gesture against him somehow. "I'm not about to lose my bar to the city for a new convention center."

And definitely not right before the holidays. Luke could picture that conversation: *Hey, Mom and Dad, I lost the pub. Merry Christmas.* And then his dad would start ranting about how his only son had always been a screw-up and didn't take his birthright seriously. Then his mom would tell his dad to stop saying things he didn't mean, all while glancing at Luke with disappointment. His sisters would weigh in by defending their older brother, which would provoke Dad more. He wouldn't defend himself because what could he say? The fact that he failed would be all that mattered. There would be a lot of whiskey drinking after the discontent and frustration had simmered and they were eating dinner. His family was like most, passively overlooking the discord to get through a meal. All future meals with his family would probably be the same.

Not happening.

"I just settled into my flower shop and I love it." Her arms swooped up in a flash to fold under her generous chest, and she stepped closer. "I don't want to give it up. I like downtown, my building, and *most* of my neighbors."

"You've been there less than a year. This pub has been in my family for generations. *Generations.*" The familiar grumbling of his stomach started and he glanced at his desk for antacids. "I will not go down without a fight."

"At least we *finally* agree on something."

She twirled on her boots—boots that were too dazzled to be called real cowgirl boots. At least her jeans looked western—sort of. It was hard to tell. Candace was a Wyomingite who probably didn't know a hard day's work.

From his vantage point, Luke had a straight line to watch her walk to the front door. And he appreciated every step the embellished back pockets on her dark jeans afforded.

. . .

Candace stomped back to her cozy flower shop, Kiss from a Rose. *That guy. Thinks he knows everything.* Of all the places she had to choose to locate her flower shop, she had to buy the one right smack dab next to Luke friggin' Carrigan.

She'd never daydreamed about kissing Luke in high school or before, she'd never written their names together in her homework notebooks, and she'd never studied his body. Until present day. Setting up Kiss from a Rose right next door to the Carrigans' family pub was pure coincidence, and one that had made her grimace internally and externally when she'd come face to face with him while painting her newly purchased walls.

"Well, well, well."

She'd heard his unmistakable tone behind her and whipped her head around so fast her neck muscles stung.

"You're stalking me, aren't you?" he'd asked.

His tall, defined build took up her doorway and stopped the sunlight from streaming through.

"Luke Carrigan," she deadpanned as her mind raced to catch up. Why would he think she was stalking him? *The bar next door.* Dammit. How had it taken her until now to piece that gem together? "Just trying to make the neighborhood a better place." She focused on his eyes, careful not to let her gaze roam. She couldn't give him any upper hand. Especially not now. *Great, just what I needed. It's bad enough I'm new to having a business of my own, but now I have to contend with Luke Carrigan? Just my luck.*

"So you're just doing the work for the real owner, then?"

"You wish," she said. "I'm here to stay. I bet it's going to suck to have someone around who won't take your crap."

If his dark brown polo hadn't fit him snug around his biceps, she might've said something nice. But it did. He'd grown up well. Time had only created a handsome man. And one who knew he was handsome. Which, sadly, wasn't totally unattractive. *What are you doing? Don't think of him like that. He's bad news. He's still bad news.*

"I don't mind at all. Because she surely doesn't give it as good as she gets it." With a proud chuckle at his own ridiculous try at a joke, he rolled from the wood door frame and ambled toward his pub. Those were the only few seconds she'd ever thought about selling her new building and setting up shop somewhere else, but the notion was just plain dumb. She would have to find a way to deal with him, just like high school.

And, just like school, they managed to stay out of each other's way unless completely necessary—which was usually in the back parking lot that their businesses shared. Seven months into a neighborly relationship, it seemed their stay-out-of-my-way truce had now ended.

She made her way through her flower shop. The year-round bright green walls, crisp white flooring, and splashes of pinks were a welcome relief to all the mahogany in Luke's dank bar. She tried to shake off the cold of winter—and Luke. The small white Christmas trees peppering her front room and cheerful ornaments hanging from the ceiling couldn't help but bring a smile to her face. The holiday magic always conjured hopefulness, possibilities—this year, however, it had brought negative tidings.

"Who was *that* hunk of hottie?" Sophie Graystone asked as she finished repotting a large butterfly palm plant. "I've seen him around. I didn't know you knew him."

"He's no one." Candace rubbed her forehead before picking up a sprig of evergreen lying on the island workstation behind the main counter. The beautiful bouquet of dark, long-stemmed red roses for the customer who was apparently *very* sorry for his actions the previous night wouldn't start itself.

"If I had a *no one* who looked like him, I wouldn't share either."

The hint of a wistful smirk diverted Candace's attention from her arrangement long enough to scowl at the longtime friend she'd met during summer vacation in college.

"I'd keep him tucked away in handcuffs." Sophie waggled her eyebrows.

"He's not mine."

"Eyes don't lie," Sophie sang in alto.

"Give me a break." If they were discussing anyone other than Luke Carrigan, she might've warmed to Sophie's suggestion. "I thought you were dating, oh, what's his face … Steve?"

"Nah. That wasn't ever really a thing." Sophie shrugged and gathered a handful of blue irises to add to the winter bouquets for the after-work crowd.

"His name is Luke." Candace tried to temper the exasperation in her voice. "He owns the pub next door. You should go introduce yourself."

Candace glanced at Sophie's outfit—a vibrant kelly-green Kiss from a Rose T-shirt paired nicely with tight, black leather leggings—a vast improvement over the tummy-baring tops she usually donned every chance the weather gave her. Candace had made "no midriffs" an employment requirement when she'd hired her red-headed friend.

"Maybe I will. Maybe I'll bop over and say hi after work. We should all go out later."

"Nope. He's *all* yours, honey." *And you're just his type—I think.*

Candace didn't have time to focus on Sophie's fixation, nor did she have time to consider Luke and his problems. She'd work on solving *her* problems as she made bouquets filled with white roses, white lilies, white button spray chrysanthemums, and the occasional red carnation.

"What's the word on the council situation?" Sophie settled on a stool at the other end of the dark granite island.

"Nothing good." Candace surveyed the list of orders to fill and tapped her black boot on the concrete floor.

"Don't beat yourself up, Ace. You tried."

She had tried. But her dad, brother, mother, and their high-powered friends had no pull to stop the train that Councilman Jeffrey Dean conducted—especially not at this juncture. This was probably the only moment in her entire life she regretted not being more involved with her family's real-estate world. "A lot of good my trying did. I was talking to Mabel…"

"Which one is that again?"

"She owns the coffee shop with the really yummy BLT. Anyway, she doesn't think she'll reopen at the new location across town."

"Take the money and run? Now that's what I'm talking about." Sophie grabbed the remote for the CD player.

"It's not about the money, Soph. It's about her business." The look in Mabel's eyes had been devastatingly sad. "They shouldn't be able to do this." Candace stuffed a white chrysanthemum into red square vase, but the pressure was too great and the stem snapped. She tossed the broken flower onto the island, briefly closed her eyes, and when she opened them her entire face felt tight. "Their reasoning doesn't even make sense. Run seven businesses out of business to try to bring more business to town? How screwed up is that?"

"Uh-oh." Sophie switched on the local rock station and low rumblings of electric guitar and drums filled the wide space.

"What?"

"I've heard that tone before."

"So?" Candace squinted at her friend.

"Ace, that's your fightin' voice." Sophie winked and played air guitar like the front woman of a band—which she happened to be for Orange Heart, an all-woman '80s cover band.

Candace smiled at her wild friend. "Well, maybe it is. I can't sit back and watch. I'm not a spectator in my own life." Especially considering the nasty rumor Blake had relayed to her. Apparently when Councilman Dean had found out she'd purchased a building in one of the two areas they were considering for the convention center site, he'd pushed hard for her street block to be chosen. *What an ass.* She stabbed another chrysanthemum into the bouquet, this time managing to keep the flower in one piece.

"So, what are you going to do?" Sophie asked while bobbing her head to the beat.

"Not move. I'll tell you that right now. This is a prime location, a block off Main Street and easy access for delivery." She shook her head and glued lace to the top of the red glass square. Her heartbeat thudded in her ears and anchored her resolve. The council wasn't going to steal her, or anyone else's, business.

"There's another way to make all your problems go away." Sophie lowered her voice. "I know a guy."

Of course she does.

"No *guys.*" She pointed at Sophie. *Not yet, anyway.* Candace blew out a deep breath of air, letting her cheeks puff in the process. "There's a city council meeting tonight. I'll start there."

Yes, her initial contacts had gotten her nowhere and Luke was pissed. So what? She'd never given up before when she wanted something and she wasn't about to start now. Nope. She was going to convince every single person at the blasted town hall meeting that the convention center needed to be built elsewhere. She'd even find a new location and point out the reasons why it was better suited for the community. *Time for my game face.*

She would go to this meeting and rock it—like a boss.

In the mood for more Crimson Romance?
Check out *Holiday Wedding* by Robyn Neeley at
CrimsonRomance.com.

Printed in the United States
By Bookmasters